"You conned me, Nick," Laura said tersely, slamming the truck's door

"Hold it right there, lady." Nick's tight muscle shirt showed off his tattoo. A coiled viper. He turned to face her.

"I didn't know if you were in on the smuggling. Anyway, it didn't work the way I'd planned. Once you were in my arms, I was a goner. I didn't care about the smuggling anymore."

Laura's anger faded. "Some spy you are," she said with a grin. "I wouldn't go into espionage work if I were you. Especially if it involves prying secrets from women."

"Woman. Just one. You. There's something about you, Laura. Maybe the way your eyes get all dark and dreamy. See, they're starting to get like that now."

She couldn't resist him. Not when she looked into his eyes and remembered how it felt to kiss him. She leaned toward Nick. He leaned toward her. And behind them, a horn blared.

The Anasazi Indians, whose culture is shrouded in mystery, have always fascinated **Vicki Lewis Thompson**. She decided to take literary license and created an Anasazi death mask as the focal element in *Anything Goes*. Who knows? Maybe such a mask does exist, buried somewhere in the walls of an unexcavated cliff dwelling in New Mexico, awaiting discovery. And, just maybe, the mask might have a mystical power. . . .

Books by Vicki Lewis Thompson

Anything Goes
VICKI LEWIS THOMPSON

Harlequin Books

TORONTO • NEW YORK • LONDON
AMSTERDAM • PARIS • SYDNEY • HAMBURG
STOCKHOLM • ATHENS • TOKYO • MILAN
MADRID • WARSAW • BUDAPEST • AUCKLAND

For Audrey and Nathan Thompson,
who have California sand in their shoes

Published May 1992

ISBN 0-373-25496-2

ANYTHING GOES

Prologue

New Mexico, 1262 A.D.

THE RHYTHM OF DRUMS and the tattoo of gourd rattles echoed in the dark canyon. Clouds covered the moon and stars. Nothing challenged the blackness until splashes of firelight began to glow in the doors and windows of a dwelling carved into a cliff high above the river. Wood smoke laced with the fragrance of herbs drifted on a night breeze.

In the central kiva lay the daughter of the clan's chieftain, courted by the spirit of death. Toward dawn, the sky began to lighten, embers flickered and cooled to gray ash. The drums and rattles stopped. Weary priests watched helplessly as the young woman struggled for breath and grew still.

In the silence, the girl's mother stepped forward, a bowl of wet clay clutched against one hip. Kneeling beside her daughter, she crooned and smoothed the soft clay carefully over the young face. Then she waited, not moving, for the rust-colored mud to dry, waited for the clay to absorb the power of the girl's soul, the power of her unrealized greatness.

The mother would paint the mask with the clan's sacred symbols and adorn it with blue-green iridescent abalone shell, more precious because it had been traded from clans who lived many days' journey to the west. Having lost her daughter, she would find comfort in the mask and make a gift of it to her clan, a gift that would punish evil and reward virtue. It would be well hidden, guarded from raiders.

When at last the mask was dry to her touch, the mother removed it slowly and stood. Holding the mask aloft, she began to chant.

1

THE CADILLAC wouldn't start. Laura jiggled the key, the steering wheel and the gas pedal. The damn engine wouldn't even turn over. Great. She leaned back with a sigh. Just her luck to be caught doing what she'd been told not to.

Atkins, the man who'd hired her to drive the car from Clovis, New Mexico, to San Francisco, had demanded she take the inland route up Interstate Five. But Laura had never seen the ocean and hadn't thought Atkins would know if she took Route One instead. Maybe he still wouldn't have to know if she called Lance for help.

She left the car in the parking lot of the seaside restaurant. As she walked toward the building to find a pay phone, she breathed deeply of the salt air spiced with the fragrance of evergreens. Her disobedience had been worth it. She'd fallen in love with the California coast, and besides, Big Sur wasn't impossibly far from San Francisco. Lance could drive down and help her figure this out—if he knew anything about cars. On the trip over from New Mexico she'd realized there were lots of things she didn't know about Lance, considering she planned to marry him someday.

She located the telephone near the entrance and dialed his number. It was busy. Frustrated, she paced the area. Passing a newspaper vending machine, she glanced through the glass at the front page. A color photograph of an ancient mask took up most of the top half of the section. Normally, Laura wouldn't have taken a second look; she wasn't all that interested in Indian artifacts. Inexplicably, something drew her closer to the vending machine and she crouched until the photo was at eye level.

The mask was of clay, powdery and bleached almost white with age. Faded symbols decorated the cheeks and forehead, and irregular pieces of abalone shell, set in the edges of the mask, shimmered in a pastel rainbow of pinks and blues. Laura gazed into the sightless eyes and knew, without understanding how, that the mask had been made for a young woman, a girl with long dark hair.... Laura struggled for the image, as if recalling a hazy dream. She felt the warmth of a fire. Straining to listen, she heard, as though carried a great distance by the wind, drumbeats. Voices chanted rhythmically in an unfamiliar language. Wood smoke tantalized her nostrils....

"Excuse me." A woman pushed past her, shoved a coin into the vending machine, grabbed a paper and strode away.

Laura felt as if someone had thrown cold water into her face. She shivered and rubbed goose bumps from her arms. What was wrong with her? For a moment the images had been so real.... She must have been alone on the road too long, she decided.

She'd been so absorbed by the picture of the mask that she hadn't even read the headline. Rare Anasazi

Artifact Stolen. The dateline for the story was Las Cruces, New Mexico. The first paragraph explained that the mask, valued at more than two million dollars, had been taken from an archaeological dig northwest of Las Cruces. Authorities believed it had been smuggled out of the state for sale to a private collector. Laura looked at the mask again and told herself it was just an old piece of clay. This business with the car not starting had jangled her nerves and fueled her imagination, that was all there was to it. She shook her head in disbelief. The mask was unusual, but two million dollars for a piece of old clay was ridiculous.

Straightening, she went to try Lance's number again.

NICK HOOPER held the phone loosely in one hand while he listened to his half brother Lance. In the other hand Nick held a beer.

"Laura won't be any trouble at all," Lance said. "Just tell her this training seminar is important to my career at the bank. She's a loan officer, too, and we've talked about becoming branch managers. She'll understand why I can't be there for the next few days. She's really terrific that way."

Nick dredged up the only image he had of Lance's girlfriend—a snapshot Lance had shown him once of Laura Rhodes, in white shorts and a black halter top, lounging against the front fender of Lance's red Toyota MR-2. Her long, dark hair hung loose past her bare shoulders and her lips were curved in a provocative smile. If Nick had had someone who looked like Laura coming to stay with him, he sure wouldn't be running off to a training seminar.

Lance interrupted his reflection. "You're bummed out, aren't you?"

"Not yet. Give me time. Right now I'm confused."

"I would have told you last night, except you were asleep when I got in from the party, and you'd left for work before I woke up this morning. I thought a phone call was better than a note."

"Marginally better." Nick took another sip of beer.

"You don't think I should be doing this, do you?"

"What I think isn't as important as what Laura will think. First you enlist her to drive some stranger's car, not knowing a damn thing about the guy except that he's a customer at your bank, and now, after she quits her job in New Mexico and takes the risk of driving out here, she arrives to find you gone. If this woman is important to you, you sure have a funny way of showing it."

He heard Lance sigh at the other end of the line. "Okay, I'll level with you. I set up the car thing partly as a favor to Atkins. He needed his Cadillac transported up here, and after I told him I'd worked in New Mexico, he decided to make use of my contacts."

"Plus it allowed you to bring your girlfriend to San Francisco for free," Nick reminded him.

"That's the part that's making me nervous. Laura's great, but I'm not so sure I'm ready to settle down yet. From the sound of her letters, she thinks we're practically engaged."

"Are you saying that you signed up for this seminar on purpose, Lance, so she won't be so sure of you?"

"In a way. I need time to think. After all, I haven't seen her in six months. That's a long time."

Nick muttered an oath. Six months wouldn't change a man's mind if he was in love, but his little brother obviously wasn't. Meanwhile this woman had given up her entire life to join him in San Francisco. When Lance had asked to come and live with him six months ago, Nick had hoped to find that his brother had grown up. Judging by this stunt, however, Lance Hooper hadn't matured.

"Listen, I have to go," Lance said. "I have some work to finish up and the airport van will be here soon. Let me give you the number of the hotel where I'll be in Seattle."

Nick fished in his jeans pocket for a pencil stub and wrote the number Lance dictated on a pad by the phone.

"I'll see you Friday, Nick. And don't worry about Laura. Everything will work out."

"Right." Nick grimaced and hung up. This was turning into one helluva day. First he'd opened the mail to discover his contractor's license application had hit another snag, and now Lance was leaving his girlfriend, or the woman who thought she was his girlfriend, for Nick to baby-sit.

He glanced around his study. He was renting the house with an option to buy and had appropriated the second floor as his private domain after Lance had moved in. His bedroom and bath were the only enclosed rooms left upstairs; he'd knocked down the remaining walls to make the large study and workroom where he spent most of his time when he was home. He'd put Lance's girlfriend downstairs, in Lance's room. Maybe he wouldn't have much contact with her, after all.

The French doors on the far wall of the study opened onto a balcony where he usually relaxed after work. Nick returned to his cushioned lounge chair and was getting comfortable, the beer can halfway to his lips, when the phone rang again. The way his luck was running, he hated to answer it, but somebody could be offering him another carpentry job. He walked back to the study, picked up the receiver and tried to sound pleasant.

"Lance?" The voice was musical, sexy.

Upon hearing it, Nick felt a jolt of awareness. He also had a premonition who the caller was. "Lance isn't here. I can take a message."

"Then you must be Nick," the woman said. "You sound a little like Lance, except now I can tell your voice is a bit deeper. This is Laura Rhodes."

"Oh, yeah," Nick said, as if just remembering. "Lance said you'd show up today." *And Lance is a damn fool not to be waiting with open arms.*

"Well, I have a small problem," she said. "When will Lance be home?"

So she'd be delayed, he thought. That was a piece of luck he hadn't counted on. He toyed with the idea of telling her about Lance's wishy-washy attitude and possibly saving her some grief, but decided he didn't really have that right. He'd play it Lance's way. "Lance won't be back for a few days. He's at a training seminar for the bank. Came up at the last minute. He said you'd understand." Nick hoped she wouldn't. Anyone with spunk would be ticked off that her boyfriend would choose a last-minute business seminar over her.

"Oh." She didn't sound pleased.

"Are you still in New Mexico?" he asked, hoping she hadn't left yet. Maybe she could retrieve her job. The temptation to tell her about Lance's cold feet grew stronger.

"Actually I'm at a restaurant in Big Sur. I stopped to have something to eat and when I came back to the car, it wouldn't start."

Nick should have known not to answer the phone. Here was trouble, and Lance, who should be handling it, was probably getting into his airport van by now. "Maybe you should notify the guy who owns the car."

"I would, except that he's...I don't know...not the sort of man who'd understand. He's sort of imposing. He wears...now this will sound silly...he wears black boots with a black widow spider stitched on them. Those boots give me the shivers."

"Maybe he just likes bugs," Nick said, wanting to reassure her. Lance should have checked the guy out. "Anyway, it's not your fault if the car broke down," Nick continued. "He can't blame you for that."

"Well, no, but I'm not supposed to be here. He told me to take Highway Five instead of the coast road, to minimize any chance of trouble."

"And instead you wanted to see the ocean," Nick guessed, admiring her independence.

"I didn't think it would matter so much, and I've never been to California before."

Nick closed his eyes. He could feel her problems reaching out to ensnare him.

"I was hoping Lance might be able to drive down and help me," she continued. "I don't know a lot about cars, and I thought maybe Lance . . ."

"Lance doesn't know a lot about cars, either."

"Oh."

He fought his sympathetic response as long as possible, knowing he'd give in eventually. He always did when someone called for help. Lance kidded him about having a "savior of the world" complex. "It could be a loose wire, something simple like that," Nick said finally. "I'll drive down and take a look."

"No, I couldn't ask that of you. We've never even met. I'll handle this. Don't worry."

Nick liked her refusal. She wasn't reacting like a clinging, abandoned female, which made him more eager to help her out. "Lance asked me to watch out for you while he was gone," he said. That wasn't precisely true, but Nick thought Lance *should* have asked him.

"I appreciate that, but I'll manage."

"Look, I'll be down in no time." He tore Lance's hotel number from the pad and stuck it into his pocket, just in case this turned into a bigger mess than he anticipated. "After all, what are big brothers for?"

"Well . . . okay." He could hear the relief in her voice as she gave him the restaurant's location. "I'll find some way to make this up to you," she added.

"Don't worry about it." Nick put down his half-full can of beer. "I wasn't doing much of anything, anyway."

LAURA REPLACED the receiver and moved aside so that the short, chubby man standing behind her could use the phone. Pausing at the newspaper rack, she decided to buy a paper to give her something to read while waiting for Nick. After a quick trip to the car for a sweatshirt, she returned to the restaurant's open-air deck and ordered coffee. At least she'd picked a gorgeous place to get stuck in, she thought, glancing out over the vast expanse of the Pacific Ocean. The restaurant, built of stone and timber, was perched on a pine-covered bluff. Below the deck, which was cantilevered out like the prow of a ship, the ocean churned against a jagged shoreline of tumbled black lava.

Shivering in the cool breeze coming off the water, Laura considered going back to the car for sweatpants to pull on over her shorts. The idea of dressing warmly in July made her smile. Clovis would be a furnace by this time of day. Working in an air-conditioned bank had helped Laura endure New Mexico, but she had always known that one day she'd find a cooler, greener place to live.

When Lance had been transferred to the bank in Clovis, he'd focused her attention on San Francisco with all his talk. He had a brother there, he'd said. The

Clovis job was temporary, and Lance had had his eye on a position in the Bay Area. Laura wondered which she'd fallen in love with first—Lance—or his dream of moving to California.

She gazed at the view a while longer, decided she could manage without the sweatpants, and turned her attention to the newspaper story about the Anasazi mask.

AT THE OTHER SIDE of the deck the short man watched until he was certain the dark-haired woman had settled in for a while, then waddled down the stairs to the indoor portion of the restaurant. He extracted a quarter from his pants pocket and shoved the coin into the slot in the pay phone.

A telephone buzzed on a rosewood desk in the lavish study of a San Francisco home. The man seated at the desk slowly put down the afternoon newspaper and waited two rings before picking up the receiver. Then he leaned back in his swivel chair and rested his ankle on his knee. He drummed his fingers on the spider and web stitched into the black leather shank of his boot. "Yeah, I'll accept the charges," he said impatiently. After listening for a moment, he slammed both booted feet to the floor and sat up straight. "Benny, don't tell me she can't get the car started. It's a brand-new car, for God's sake!"

Benny continued talking, then the man interrupted. "I can't believe this is so screwed up! First she drives on the wrong road, where you can't watch her, and now she's stuck. The longer this takes, the better the chance

Robles will find out what's going on and come after the mask.... She what? Please don't tell me she called a tow truck. We don't want that car in some frigging garage where they— She did? Hooper's brother? Didn't know he had one. Maybe this will work out, after all."

He leaned forward and gripped the desk. "Listen, Benny, here's what you do. Get her to let you look under the hood. Maybe a wire's loose or something. Yeah, I *know* I told you to keep a low profile, but it's too late for that. Robles is probably on her tail by now. And stop whining to me about Robles. If he decides to take you out, you'll never know what hit you. It'll be painless, so quit worrying. And Benny, stop calling goddamned *collect!*" The man slammed down the receiver.

A moment later he picked it up again and punched out a new number. "Get me Lance Hooper. He is? What airline?" Without bothering to say goodbye, the man pushed the Disconnect button and flipped his Rolodex. Shortly he had the next number dialed. "You have a passenger by the name of Lance Hooper," he told the person at the other end. "Page him." While he waited, he tapped a pen against his boot. When the line clicked open, he straightened in his chair.

"Hooper? Atkins here. Your sweet young thing took the blessed coast road instead of the interstate and got her little fanny stuck at Big Sur.... I don't know. Car won't start. Benny thinks your brother's on his way down. You say anything about this to him?" The man rolled his eyes as Hooper defended himself. "Okay, okay. Just asking. Now get over here.... Who cares about that? Who cares a rat's ass about your precious seminar? You shouldn't be out of town at a time like this, anyway. What's the matter, yuppie boy, afraid of getting your pinkies dirty?" Atkins laughed. "Get over here, Hooper. Now." He clicked the receiver back into its cradle and rubbed his eyes. It was turning into one helluva day.

LAURA BECAME ABSORBED in the article about the stolen mask. It had been intended for a museum in San Francisco. Such thefts were common; there was a thriving black market, but most finds weren't as significant as this one. Archaeologists from the University of New Mexico had told reporters the mask probably had something to do with a burial ritual, one that had never been discovered until now. Although experts had placed a monetary value on the artifact, on-site archaeologists considered it a priceless find.

Finishing the story, Laura glanced over the rest of the front-page news before turning to her horoscope. It warned her to beware of strangers and to use caution when traveling. She laughed and turned to the advice columns.

"Excuse me."

She glanced up. The short, chubby man was approaching her table. Her first thought was that he could be Nick, although this wasn't the way she'd pictured him. Besides, it was way too early for Nick to arrive.

"Excuse me," the stranger said again, "but is that your tan Cadillac in the parking lot?"

"Am I blocking your way? You see, it won't start, and . . ."

"I know," the man said, fiddling with the ends of a silver-and-turquoise bola tie. "I think I can help."

Laura hesitated. Having Nick look at the car was one thing, but this person was a total stranger. She didn't really believe in horoscope messages, but thought about the warning. "Thanks for offering, but help's on the way." Laura smiled to avoid hurting his feelings. The guy looked harmless enough. He was shorter than she was, and his face was as pink as a baby's.

"We could take a look, anyway," he suggested, his expression eager. "Yeah, that's it. Let's take a look."

Laura tried not to laugh. Maybe the guy was infatuated with her or something. "Thanks, but I'll be fine. My friend is driving down."

His eyes narrowed. "Can he fix cars?"

"I certainly hope so."

"Well!" He clapped his hands and rubbed them together. "What if we have it fixed when your friend gets here? Wouldn't that be great?"

His persistence was getting on Laura's nerves. She was glad there were a few customers lingering at the other tables, and the occasional waitress. "I appreciate the offer, but I prefer to wait for my friend," she said more firmly.

"Hmm, well, I don't think you should wait alone. How about me waiting with you? What do you have there, coffee? Would you like some more? I could have a cup, too. We could have a cup together. We could—"

"Look," she said, breaking into his monologue. "I don't mean to be rude, but I'm doing fine by myself."

"I only thought I could buy you a cup of coffee." The man's round face sagged comically.

Laura decided there was only one way to get rid of this man. "I'm spoken for," she said softly. "My boyfriend is on his way here, and I wouldn't want him to see me with someone else." She grimaced. "He's the jealous type."

The man looked at her a moment longer, nodded, and walked to another table. Laura brought the newspaper up in front of her and kept it there as a barrier. Every time she peeked around it, the guy was still watching her. By her count he consumed at least four desserts, and she became convinced that he wouldn't leave until she did.

The time dragged, but at last Laura glanced toward the steps leading down to the parking lot and saw a man of medium height and wavy brown hair. A denim work shirt spanned his broad shoulders and his worn Levi's jeans bore traces of sawdust at the knees.

Leaving the newspaper on the table, Laura grabbed her purse and jumped up. She'd stage a convincing scene for her chubby friend. "Nick!" she called and rushed toward him. "I'm so glad you're here. I've really missed you." She threw her arms around his neck.

"Laura?"

"Yep." He had little choice but to hug her back, she knew. She would have given a month's pay for a picture of his astonished expression. "Pretend you're really glad to see me," she muttered, looking into his gray eyes. "I'm trying to get rid of that chubby guy over by the railing. I told him you were my boyfriend."

Nick arched one eyebrow, glanced at the man and studied him briefly. Then his gaze returned to Laura's face and he smiled. "Okay," he said, and kissed her.

2

LAURA RETURNED THE KISS with faked enthusiasm at first, thinking only to fool the pudgy man, but she began enjoying herself as Nick's lips moved over hers with gentle assurance. He was just tall enough for their bodies to fit together as if intended for this particular activity. He took his time and held her firmly while the musky scent of sawdust and elemental male drifted pleasantly around her. Arousal nudged at her, teasing her with images of making love with Nick Hooper. His kiss told her that he knew very well how to proceed.

She realized dimly that she had no business taking pleasure in a kiss from the brother of the man she planned to marry, yet the sweet pressure of Nick's mouth and the warmth of his embrace were the best things that had happened to her in a long time. Dreamily she relaxed in his arms. He seemed to sense her abandonment and pulled her closer. His tongue edged inside her mouth to begin a leisurely exploration that made her heart beat wildly in response. Her reaction was growing dangerous, yet she couldn't pull away.

At last Nick was the one to call a halt. He eased out of the kiss as naturally as he'd eased into it and gazed at her. His breathing seemed a bit labored, but otherwise his expression was calm. "How was that?"

She swallowed. "Wonderful."

His gray eyes warmed with amusement. "Do you suppose we fooled your friend?"

She couldn't imagine what he was talking about. Then she remembered. She'd forgotten the pudgy man, forgotten about everything except kissing Nick. Startled, she moved out of his arms. "I'm sure we fooled him," she murmured, looking away. "Thanks."

"No problem. Shall we take a look at the car?"

"Sure." She still couldn't meet his gaze and knew she was blushing. What must he think of her? She was practically engaged to his brother, and she'd just kissed him as if she'd be perfectly willing to . . .

"We'd better keep up the pretense," Nick said, hooking an arm around her shoulders and guiding her down the wooden stairs to the parking lot. "Did the guy try to pick you up or something?"

"I'm not sure that's what he had in mind, but he was very persistent about wanting to help with the car." Laura resisted the urge to snuggle closer to Nick. She didn't believe in instant attractions, but something strange was happening to her.

"Maybe he was just being a good Samaritan." Nick glanced at her bare legs. "But I doubt it. I'm glad you didn't take his offer. The parking lot is more secluded than the restaurant, and he might have felt free to try something." They reached the bottom of the steps and he released her. "Okay now?"

She faced him. "I'm fine. Listen, Nick, about what just happened, I—"

"Wait a minute. If anyone should apologize, it's me. You're under stress, and you probably miss Lance. I had no right to take advantage of that, but..." He shrugged. "What can I say?" He stared straight into her eyes. "That kiss felt really good, Laura, and I forgot for a minute that you belong to Lance. I won't forget again."

Desire stirred within her and Laura realized with dismay that she half wanted Nick to forget. What a mess. "It's not your fault. I threw myself into your arms."

"You notice I didn't throw you back out again."

"No. It was a dumb idea on my part, though. I'm sorry."

"Don't be."

She stood there wishing he'd kiss her again and knowing he wouldn't—and she shouldn't want him to. He was right; stress and missing Lance explained her reaction. Not that he looked enough like Lance for her to confuse the two. After all, they were only half brothers, with the same father but not the same mother, so they wouldn't necessarily look alike. Lance was tall and slim, with jet-black hair and a nonchalant slouch to his walk. Nick was shorter, more muscular, *nicer to hold*. "Anyway, I don't know that I *belong* to Lance," she said. "That sounds like medieval terminology."

"Okay, then let's just say he saw you first, and the two of you have talked about marriage. I don't poach on my brother's territory."

"There you go again. I'm not *territory*, either."

Nick threw up his arms. "All right. You're free and your own person. You can kiss anybody you want, whenever you want. Shall we try it again?"

Oh, she was tempted. "Better not."

"Didn't think so." He folded his arms. "However you want to phrase it, you're off-limits to me, Laura Rhodes. Since we'll be living alone together for four days, we'd better get that straight. The kiss was dynamite, but it was the first and last one of that kind we'll exchange. Agreed?"

"Agreed." She liked the character lines in his face. Lance had always looked so young, younger even than his twenty-seven years. According to him, Nick was older by seven years, making him thirty-four. He looked as if he'd seen a bit of the world; there was maturity in his expression, depth to his gaze.

"Let's see what we can do with this boat so we can get you back on your way." He walked to his truck. It was white, with a metal rack welded to the back and Hooper Carpentry lettered on the cab door. "I brought my battery tester," he said over his shoulder. "Can you put up the hood of the car?"

"Sure." Laura unlocked the door and slid into the passenger seat. She reached under the dashboard and fumbled for a latch, but found nothing. Nick retrieved the tester and waited; she groped around and felt increasingly foolish. "I can't find the latch," she said. "I've never had to put up the hood before."

He crouched beside the driver's door. "Should be right under here." He reached in and his arm brushed her bare thigh. "Sorry."

She concentrated on calming her pulse rate, telling herself that circumstances had caused her to react this way. She edged away from him, but despite her evasive movements, his shoulder pressed against her hip. His head was practically in her lap. She fought the urge to run her fingers through his hair and down the back of his head. His hair had recently been cropped at the nape; a strip of skin along the hairline was sunburned to a tender pink.

"I can't find it, either." He extricated himself and settled on his heels. "Got a manual in the glove compartment?"

"Maybe. I never looked." She leaned over the passenger seat and caught a glimpse of the chubby man at the top of the stairs. "That guy's still hanging around."

Nick turned his head and saw the man retreat to the deck. "He's waiting to see if I'll leave and he'll have another chance."

"Don't leave."

"I won't."

She opened the glove compartment, feeling guilty about causing Nick all this trouble, but couldn't think of any other options. "Here." She handed him the manual. "I won't forget what you've done for me."

He shrugged and flipped open the booklet. "I won't ask for much. Just your firstborn child."

"You'll be out of luck there. Lance doesn't want children."

"Yeah, I've heard him say that, too." He glanced up and studied her for a moment. "Do you?"

"I hadn't thought about it much. I've been concentrating more on moving to California and continuing my banking career. Why?"

"I don't know. Idle curiosity, I guess."

Laura didn't believe, even after knowing him such a short time, that Nick felt "idly curious" about anything. If he asked a question, he had a reason.

He returned his attention to the manual. "Be careful about Lance. If you let him, he'll run your life."

"Brotherly advice?"

"Yeah. Okay, here it is. The hood latch is a button in the glove compartment," he said, standing. "I'll keep this out for future reference."

"In the glove compartment?" Laura found the button and pressed it, releasing the hood. "What a place for it! We could have looked all day."

"I've had worse assignments." He winked at her, then walked to the front of the car.

It took Laura a minute to realize he'd just flirted with her. "Hey!" she called. "If we're off-limits to each other, what are you doing, making remarks like that?"

He looked up with the startled expression of a little boy caught stealing a cookie.

"You were flirting."

"You're right."

"That's not fair."

"Right again." His grin was sheepish.

"Well?" She put her hands upon her hips and stared at him.

He braced both arms against the radiator and returned her stare. "This is going to be a tough four days."

"I could stay somewhere else until Lance gets home."

"That's dumb. You'd be spending money unnecessarily."

"Would I?"

"Yes." Nick sighed. "I can control my impulses, but it would sure help if you'd find something else to wear besides those shorts."

"A suit of chain mail?"

He chuckled. "That would be nice."

Laura smiled in spite of herself. "I'll see what I can dig up." Leaving him to tinker, she opened the trunk and took the sweatpants out of her suitcase. Of all the things she'd imagined about coming to California, being attracted to Lance's brother hadn't been one of them. And Nick was attracted to her, too. Maybe if she hadn't pulled that dumb stunt with the kiss, they'd have started off on a more platonic note. But they had kissed, and obviously neither of them could forget it.

She tugged the sweatpants on over her shorts then walked to the front of the car. Did Nick have a girlfriend? He certainly didn't act like a man committed to someone, but he probably had dates. "You know, if you ever want me to clear out of the apartment for the evening, let me know," she said.

"I will." He grunted softly as he twisted something. "Try the key."

She did, but the engine remained silent. "I'd hate to think you canceled dates or anything because I'm going to be there," she called from the front seat.

"When you get an idea, you won't let it go, will you?"

"I just . . ."

"Believe me, I haven't canceled a single date because of you, Laura. But before we find out if you'll be a hindrance to my love life, we have to get you to San Francisco, and that doesn't look promising right now."

She scrambled out of the car to stand beside him. "You're giving up?"

"Afraid so. I think your problem has to do with the computer, and I'm not qualified to fool with that. You'll have to arrange for a tow, after all."

Her stomach knotted. She'd been so convinced that Nick would save the day, and now she'd have to call Atkins and admit that she wouldn't deliver the car on time. "Okay," she said letting her shoulders slump. "I hate to ask, but could you at least stay until the tow truck gets here? I'm still nervous about that guy."

He tightened a hose connection. "What do you mean? I'm staying with you until the car's fixed."

"You can't do that. You have work to do, I'm sure."

"I do, but Joanne's kitchen cabinets can wait."

"I don't want you to make one of your customers angry."

"If Joanne wants to fire me because I took time off for an emergency, I don't want her business."

"I hope you can afford that kind of independence," Laura said. Nick was quite a contrast to Lance, who turned himself inside out to please customers.

He grimaced. "So do I. Unfortunately it's the only way I know how to work."

"Maybe the tow-truck driver will be able to fix it and we can both be on our way."

"Maybe. And I still might be able to find the problem, but it'll be getting dark in a couple of hours. I'll keep trying while you call someone. We can always cancel the tow if I get lucky. You probably should notify the guy who owns the car, too."

"Okay." She hesitated.

"Want me to come with you?" He glanced up. "I could leave this for a—"

"No," she interrupted. "Of course not. I'll be fine."

Nick smiled. "If he shows up, holler loud. I'll be there in a flash. But I think you're safe inside with other people around. Maybe while you're gone I'll find the magic solution to starting the car."

"I'll be right back," she said, and walked off. "And Nick," she added, turning back to him. "I'm not a wimp."

"I never thought for a moment that you were."

His smile stayed with her as she crossed the parking lot to the restaurant. She wondered if she was still being influenced by the circumstances. When Lance got back from his seminar, she'd be honest with him. He might be disappointed after he'd taken all this trouble to bring her over here, but it was better to face the problem of her attraction to Nick right away than sweep it under the rug.

NICK WATCHED until Laura was safely inside before looking at the engine again. He adjusted another wire and moved to the driver's seat to try the key again. No luck. Frustrated, he started pushing buttons—windows, door locks, gas-tank cover. The window on the passenger side rolled halfway down and stopped.

Nick tried it again. The same thing happened, as if it were hitting something. At least he'd found something he might be able to fix. He couldn't imagine that a jammed window had anything to do with the car not starting, but he'd take the door panel off, anyway, just for the satisfaction of doing something useful.

In a short time he had the panel off. It took him a minute to figure out what he was looking at, but it was obvious that the obstruction that prevented the window from working properly had been put there on purpose. A brown package was braced inside the door with strips of wood. Nick's first thought was drugs. His second was that Lance could be in on it; even Laura could. Holy heaven! Nick hadn't a clue as to what he was dealing with here, except that it was bad.

He thought fast, watching the restaurant door to see if Laura was coming out. The tow truck was on its way. Someone could find this, and if Lance was involved, he'd be in big trouble. Nick wished he didn't suspect his brother, but after living with him for six months, Nick knew it was possible. The stupid jerk might think this was a great way to make big bucks. He might even have convinced Laura. But Nick didn't want to believe Laura was a smuggler. Hell, he didn't want to think Lance was! If Lance had knowingly become part of some drug-running scheme, Nick would skin him alive. But until he knew for sure, he had to try to protect his little brother from his own stupidity.

Nick eased out the parcel and replaced the door panel as fast as he could, glancing around every few seconds to check for Laura's return. Grabbing his screwdriver, he carried the package to his truck and yanked open the driver's door. Lucky he was handy with tools, he thought, crouching to remove the six screws that held the air vent in place.

He sniffed the package before stashing it inside the vent. Sure didn't smell like drugs, but he'd bet his last dollar it was contraband of some kind. As he tightened the last screw, he heard Laura's voice behind him.

"Don't tell me something's wrong with your truck?" she asked.

Had she seen him? He hoped to God not. "Stiff clutch pedal," he said, inventing an excuse. He got to his feet and turned to face her. Every time he looked at Laura he thought of that kiss, and something besides his clutch pedal grew stiff. He had a hard time believing she was a drug smuggler as she stood before him in the soft twilight, her cinnamon-brown eyes clear and innocent, her lips full and inviting. Yet a drug smuggler she might be. "Any luck with the phone calls?"

She made a face. "Atkins wasn't thrilled to hear that his car will be delayed until tomorrow."

I'll bet, Nick thought. "So he can take a cab for another day."

"That's what I said to him. I don't know why he's so bent out of shape, except, of course, I wasn't supposed to be on this road."

All sorts of crazy possibilities ran through Nick's mind. This fellow Atkins might not be in on the smuggling at all. Laura could have had this idea all by herself. Maybe the stalled car was part of the scam. On the other hand, if someone was supposed to pick up the stash from this parking lot, Nick had already ruined that. "How about a tow truck?" he asked, wondering if even the towing company could be in on the deal. Anything was possible.

"The cashier recommended somebody. They'll be out in about half an hour."

"Good." He decided that if Laura knew about whatever had been concealed in the door, and all this was part of some grand plan, then she was one hell of a liar. He'd find out, one way or the other. "Did you run into our pudgy friend?" Nick had some new ideas about that guy, too. He might be after the stash, not Laura.

"As a matter of fact, he was hanging around by the phone, but he didn't bother me or anything."

"Glad to hear it." Nick was relieved. The guy apparently hadn't seen him transfer the goods.

"The guy was listening when I talked to Atkins, so I made it sound as if you'd be staying with me until the car's fixed, but you don't really have to, Nick. If you'll just hang around until the truck comes, I'll ask them to give me a lift into Monterey."

"And then what?"

She shrugged. "I'll find a motel. Nobody will be able to fix the car until morning, but that's my problem. No need for you to be put out, too."

"Laura, I wouldn't dream of letting you stay by yourself." *Not until I know what the hell is going on.* He turned toward the stairs where a rounded figure was visible for a moment before melting back into the shadows. "You're too much of a target." *A huge understatement.*

"I really hate to put you through all this trouble, Nick."

"As I said before, that's what big brothers are for."

"Well, if you insist."

Her smile warmed places inside him that he'd never even realized were cold. "I insist." He knew where he'd take her. He also knew he'd make up a story that there was only one room left. He wasn't letting Laura Rhodes out of his sight. Before the night was over, he'd know whether or not she was involved in something illegal.

3

THE MAN LEANED BACK in his leather swivel chair and propped his black boots on top of the rosewood desk. He was careful not to mar the boots or the gleaming surface, but wanted to establish his authority. He smoothed his mustache before he spoke to the man sitting across from him. "Your girlfriend and that meddling brother of yours have called a tow truck, Hooper. That means the Caddy will be in some yard all night. I don't want that. Go get the mask for me."

Lance hunched his narrow shoulders. "Get it, Mr. Atkins? How?"

"Climb the fence." He pushed a key across the desk. "This will get you into the car without setting off the alarm system. I told you where I had that body-shop man hide the mask. Take a screwdriver and get the thing out of there."

"But . . ."

"Don't give my your 'buts.' You said your girlfriend would be the perfect one to drive that car up here. You said she was small-town, easy to manipulate, would do what she was told. First thing I know, Benny calls me and says she's on the coast road instead of the interstate. Next thing she's stuck at Big Sur. Now the car's being towed to a wrecking yard until morning. One screwup after another. I've had to call my client and tell him his shipment will be delayed. He's not happy. A boat leaves for Hong Kong in two days. The mask has to be on it."

"I'm sorry about all this, but I didn't think Laura would—"

"Yeah, well, that proves you don't know her so good. Seems she's got her own ideas about doing things, and that means headaches for me. I want the mask up here in the morning, Hooper."

"What about Benny?" Lance was whining now. "He's already down there. Why can't he do it?"

Atkins raised his hand and held up one finger. "In the first place, Benny's not built for climbing fences. You are." He held up another finger. "In the second place, Benny is married to my sister, and she'll kill me if anything happens to him. I'm not taking that kind of risk with Benny. In the fourth place—"

"Third."

"Yeah." Atkins looked at his two fingers and put up another digit. "Third. In the third place, I asked Benny to keep an eye on your girlfriend and your brother. He can't do that if he has to get the mask and bring it up here."

"Why keep an eye on Nick and Laura? They don't know anything."

"Because." Atkins smoothed his mustache again. "I have to cover all the angles. You could have told your girlfriend about the mask. She might be doing all this on purpose, to throw me off. This could be a double cross." He glared at Lance.

"No, I didn't tell her. I swear. Laura doesn't know a thing. She thinks she's driving this car to San Francisco for you. That's all."

"And your brother?"

"I didn't tell him, either. What's the matter? Don't you trust me, Mr. Atkins?"

The man lowered his boots to the floor and leaned across the desk in a deliberately slow motion. "In two words, no."

NICK LOCKED HIS TRUCK and he and Laura walked back to the Cadillac.

"I take it that since you were working on your truck, you've given up on the car," Laura said.

"I've checked for all the usual problems. I think it must be the computer."

"You're probably right." Now that the tow truck was on the way and she'd endured Atkins's wrath, she didn't see much point in Nick wasting time on the Cadillac. "By the way, I like your license plate," she commented. "HAMMER. That's appropriate, although I suppose most carpenters use nail guns these days."

"I don't unless I absolutely have to. Power equipment is necessary when you need to save time, but I still enjoy the feel of a good hand tool. Stubborn, I guess." He glanced at her. "We've got some time before the truck arrives. What do you say I buy you a drink? You look as if you could use one."

Laura nodded. The angry accusations she'd heard from Atkins still rattled around in her mind and she felt a bit guilty at having ignored his instructions. Besides,

a drink might help ease the tension of the long afternoon.

He chose a cozy area downstairs instead of the deck,
which had become too cool for sitting. Laura ordered
a glass of a local white wine and Nick, explaining that
he still had to drive, had a soft drink. Laura's respect
for him rose another notch.

The wine relaxed her and she found herself telling
Nick about growing up in Clovis as a protected only
child, feeling smothered by her parents' constant con-
cern. They'd tried to persuade her to stay and settle
down in Clovis, but she'd been determined to strike out
on her own. Meeting Lance had provided the catalyst
for making that change.

"He was the first person I'd met in quite a while who
had big plans," she said.

"He's always had big plans." Nick drained his glass.
"Lance hopes to be rich someday."

"Perhaps." Laura discovered she didn't want to talk
about Lance. "What about you? Are you happy having your own carpentry business?"

"Yes, for now. I have ambitions to do other things, if
that's what you mean. I'll bet you do, too. What are
your dreams, Laura? Do you want to be rich, like
Lance?"

"I suppose everyone would like to have more money."
She noticed he'd turned aside her question about himself, but she didn't feel right pressing for more details.
She'd already interfered with Nick's time; she had no
right to pry into his personal life, too. Just because she'd

found it easy to tell him about herself didn't mean he had to return the gesture.

Nick studied her. "How much does that mean to you, having more money?"

She laughed. "Is this a test?"

"No. Sorry if it sounded like that. I guess I was wondering, since I know how much Lance cares about money, if you felt the same. If so, then the two of you are all set."

"You don't share his value system," Laura guessed, "and you wonder if I do."

"Something like that."

"Let's put it this way." She liked Nick and was flattered that he cared enough to ask about her values. "I don't see anything wrong with having money. Life can be easier if you don't have to worry about bills all the time, and I wouldn't mind having that sense of security. But I wouldn't compromise my idea of what's right in order to get it."

He nodded. "I'd agree with that answer."

"I think Lance might say the same thing."

"Do you?"

"Of course. Don't you?"

Nick shrugged and tossed some money onto the table. "The tow truck should be here any minute. Let's wait in the parking lot."

"Nick, let me pay for this." Laura fumbled in her purse.

He put his hand over hers. "No."

"But . . ."

"I invited you for a drink. When you invite me, then you can pay."

There it was again, the ease of manner that charmed her so. With Nick there was no superfluous movement, no unnecessary talk. Next to Nick's maturity and confidence, Lance seemed like a kid. Would a time come when she could invite Nick for a drink? Probably not. She sighed and followed him out of the restaurant.

The tow truck arrived, but the driver had no more success in starting the car than Laura or Nick had had. Soon they were following the flatbed around the curves of Big Sur to Monterey. They waited until the Cadillac had been securely locked inside a fenced enclosure patrolled by Dobermans. The driver assured them the car would be towed to the Cadillac dealership for repairs in the morning.

"Now for a meal and a good night's sleep," Nick said as he turned his truck down Abrego Street. "I know a great place we can stay, if they have room. We might have some trouble, considering how late it is."

"At this point I'd settle for anything." Laura had retrieved her overnight bag from the car, but had decided to leave the rest. A razor-wire-topped fence and two guard dogs seemed like plenty of protection for her belongings. With the combination of the wine and the leisurely ride to Monterey she was getting sleepy.

"Here we are," Nick told her. "And the Vacancy sign's still lit. You can't see the water from here, but most of the places with a view are a lot more expensive and probably booked."

"This is fine, Nick." Laura lazily admired the white buildings, the Spanish tile roofs and the brilliant pink of bougainvillea blossoms. When she rolled down her window, the air smelled of summer roses.

"If you'll stay with the truck I'll see what they have available."

"Okay." She liked his assurance. She'd told him to drive home and leave her in Monterey, but would have been devastated if he had. Despite her determination to be independent, she'd been thrown off balance by the stalled car and the strange little fat man.

Nick reappeared and walked to her side of the truck. "Only one room left."

"Too bad." Her weariness increased at the prospect of driving around town, looking for motel rooms.

"I guess we can try other places, but the desk clerk warned me that the cheaper ones won't be available. This is the height of the season."

"What should we do?"

"Well . . ."

Laura grew more alert. Was he thinking they ought to share this room? She knew a dangerous situation when she saw one, knew she shouldn't be in the same bedroom alone with Nick, not when she reacted to him as she had. "What kind of beds are in it?"

"One king." His expression was veiled.

"This sounds like a scene from a movie, Nick. Are you sure they don't have a spare broom closet somewhere for one of us?"

He shook his head. "Want to try somewhere else?"

She thought about it. She definitely didn't want to drag all over Monterey, looking for two rooms. Here was a perfectly good room in a nice place. Maybe it would work, after all. Staying in the same room would simply require mental discipline. "We should be able to handle this, Nick," she said, with a shade more confidence than she felt. "We'll be under the same roof for the next three nights, so we'll have to deal with a similar situation, anyway."

"I suppose."

"And we're both too tired to let it bother us."

"Probably."

"Then let's act like two adults and do the expedient thing. Take the room."

He paused for a minute. "Okay," he said at last. "I will."

NICK CHECKED THEM IN and drove to their assigned parking space in silence. *Don't open your mouth and spoil it, Hooper,* he thought. *You've almost got her in the net.*

From the passenger seat Laura observed Nick's tight expression. He was obviously not happy to be trapped into taking care of her.

Nick turned off the motor and glanced at Laura. Damn, she looked uncertain, as if she might change her mind. He grabbed her overnight bag from the seat between them. "I'll just run this up and then we'll get something to eat at a coffee shop I spotted down the street," he said quickly. Before she could answer, he was out the door of the truck with her bag. *She has to come back with me.* He took the keys.

He's such a gentleman, she thought, watching him hurry up the stairs to their second-floor room.

Nick deposited the bag in the room. Maybe it would be better if he separated her from the truck for a while, in case she knew where he'd hidden the stash. He loped down the steps and opened her door. "The coffee shop's close by. Let's walk."

"Sure." Laura liked his suggestion. Lance had insisted on driving his red sports car everywhere, even if they were going only a couple of blocks. "It'll feel good to stretch my legs," she said as they headed down the street. "I've been like a prisoner in that car."

Nick tensed. A prisoner? The term came so easily to her lips. "Well, we're in the exercise yard now," he said.

She laughed, glad he was relaxed enough to make jokes. "We'd better be careful, then," she said, determined to keep their conversation light. "It seems like that's where all the foul play takes place. At least in the movies."

"We'll be careful." *You don't know how careful, sweetie pie.* He ushered her inside. He asked for a corner booth in a deserted section of the restaurant, and after they were seated, suggested Laura have another glass of wine. "It'll help you relax," he said. He'd order as many glasses as it took to loosen her tongue.

He's so considerate, Laura thought. But wine was the last thing she needed when Nick presented her with such temptation. "I'm really fine now," she replied. "Wine will just muddle my brain."

That's what I want. He could see he'd have to take a different tack. "It's a gutsy thing you've done, driving all this way by yourself in somebody else's car."

"I was highly motivated to get out of Clovis, Nick," she reminded him with a smile.

"And join Lance." He had to keep her on track.

"I suppose so." She glanced away, serious again. Lance might have been her motivation before, but she wasn't so eager to see him again, now that she'd met Nick. She was glad when their meal arrived and gave her an excuse to concentrate on something else. She made a big deal out of mixing sour cream and chives into her baked potato.

Nick watched her work on the potato. She was stalling, hiding something, no doubt about it. "That's a great technique you have," he observed. "I could use you on the job for mixing putty."

She looked up. "Are you making fun of me?"

"Not really," he said, using his most sincere smile. "But from the way you're grinding away at that potato, I wonder if you're as calm as you claim to be."

Laura put down her fork and took a sip of her iced tea. Nick was seeing right through her. "Well, it has been quite a day."

He'd better not press too hard or he'd blow it. "I'll agree with that." He took a spoonful of his chili.

Laura began to eat her halibut. Maybe they'd be better off not talking at all. Before long, Nick was liable to find out how attracted she was to him—and how much she was beginning to regret her entanglement with his brother.

She's bogged down. I have to keep her talking. Nick thought fast. "You know, sometimes when we want something a lot, our judgment gets skewed," he said.

She glanced at him warily. Had he been reading her mind? "That's true."

"Sometimes we do things we wish we hadn't, make commitments we wish we hadn't." *That was masterful, Hooper.*

"Sometimes." She concentrated on her plate. His perception was uncanny. "But I believe in carrying through with commitments after I make them."

"Sometimes honoring the wrong commitment can ruin your life, Laura." He had her now. Any minute now she'd spill the whole sordid story.

She looked into his eyes. They were so gentle, so persuasive. Her heart pounded. Was he implying that she'd be better off without Lance? Did he mean she'd be better off with him, instead? He'd asked her about children. In truth, she did want them, but had assumed she could change Lance's mind. And in their discussion about money, Nick seemed to think Lance was overly concerned about wealth. What exactly was Nick trying to say? "What do you mean, ruin my life?" she asked.

Nick decided to play his trump card. "Let me give you an example. When I was seventeen and Lance was ten, he seemed to be getting all my dad's and my stepmother's attention. The guy had tennis lessons, piano lessons, riding lessons. I was too old to start that stuff but I wanted them to notice me, or if not them, at least someone. Anyone. I joined a gang."

"You *what?*"

"Lance never told you about that?"

Laura shook her head and stared at him. Lance had mentioned that his mother and father had both died two years ago, leaving Nick as his only close relative. Other than that he hadn't said much about his older brother. "You mean a street gang, with guns and knives and—?"

"Knives, yes." He touched a faint white line about two inches long on his chin. "This is one little souvenir I have from those days."

"Nick, I just can't believe this. Here you are, so clean-cut, so law-abiding, so *nice.*"

He picked up his coffee and blew the steam from the surface. He was getting just the effect he'd wanted. "Try picturing me with hair down to my shoulders, a bandanna around my head, leather jacket, pants and boots, and riding a Harley Davidson motorcycle." He sipped his coffee. "I'd probably have scared you more than your friend Atkins does."

Laura felt very young and inexperienced. Here she'd been complaining about being overprotected by her parents. At least she hadn't been ignored, hadn't turned to violence. "What happened? What changed you back?"

"The gang graduated from knives to guns."

Laura shuddered. "Then you didn't...that is, you've never..."

"Carried a gun? For a while I did. Then I saw a friend get shot and I used whatever sense I had left to leave the gang. I was in it for three years."

"You could have been killed." Laura was appalled. Nick's late father and stepmother had showered attention upon Lance and nearly lost Nick in the process.

"Or killed someone else. But anyway, the point I wanted to make is that I had a hard time deciding to leave. Crazy as it sounds, I felt I'd made a commitment to those thugs." He paused to let his point sink in. "I'd promised to be a brother for life."

She hurried to his defense, on his side all the way. "That's not a commitment, not when you were so young and impressionable, when all you wanted was to get some attention."

"Exactly. Sometimes we make foolish commitments. I've made my share. Maybe you have, too."

Laura was mesmerized by the intense look in his eyes. Nick wanted her to rethink her commitment to Lance, and there could be a very personal reason for that. He could want her himself. The realization made her tremble.

"I'm here if you need me," he said, holding his breath. "You can tell me anything, Laura. Anything at all."

She swallowed. "I . . . have to have some time to think."

He tried not to let his disappointment show. "Sure. Just don't take too long. Situations can get out of hand very quickly."

"I know." Boy, did she know. She wondered how on earth she'd stay in that room alone with him tonight, wanting him, knowing that he was encouraging her to leave Lance. She needed to get away from him for a minute. "If you'll excuse me," she said, sliding out of their booth, "I think I'll visit the ladies' room."

She left the table on unsteady feet. Good thing she hadn't had any wine, or she'd be more addled than she was already. She slipped through the rest-room door and held her palms to her heated cheeks. Perhaps Nick's revelation about his past should have made her less trusting, but instead it gave him even more credibility. He'd been through hell and come out the other side. He'd been tested and he'd beaten the odds.

A man like that knew how short life could be, how important every minute was. Why had she been so attracted to Lance? She didn't believe she was a fickle sort of woman who traded men easily. Her need to get out of Clovis had overshadowed her judgment and drawn her to an unsuitable man. Yet without Lance she'd never have met Nick, and Nick seemed to be everything she'd ever wanted. Yet she'd known him only a few hours. How could she be so sure?

Perhaps Nick was also telling her subtly that they were foolish to waste time. They both knew that Lance was wrong for her. Fate had thrown them together. Was it noble—or foolish—for them to stay apart? As Laura thought about Nick, about his strong arms and gentle lips, the struggle to remain noble seemed less and less important.

NICK DECIDED to make use of Laura's sudden departure. He slid out of the booth and hurried toward the public phones. She was on the brink of confessing everything. Although he usually hated to talk about his past, in this case it had been worth it. Soon she'd tell him about the smuggling operation, and he'd know whether Lance was involved or not. In the meantime, maybe he'd get something out of little brother. He took the plastic calling card out of his wallet, pulled the Seattle hotel's number from his jeans pocket and dialed.

When he hung up, he leaned against the wall. After talking to the registration clerk and the seminar director, Nick was convinced that Lance had canceled his trip. Nick could only imagine one possible reason. Lance was up to his neck in this smuggling thing.

Nick put in a quick call to the house and got the machine. No messages from Lance. Nick left one for him to call the Monterey hotel at once. Then he glanced at the door to the women's rest room, about thirty feet down the hall from where he stood. Laura must still be in there; she hadn't passed him to return to the table.

Maybe she'd climbed out the window. If she knew how to hot-wire his truck, she could be on her way to meet Lance by now. Maybe she had figured out that Nick had hidden the stash in the air vent. He'd thought he'd been so smart, but she could have been standing quietly behind him, watching until she decided it was time to speak up and make her presence known.

Some tough character he was. He'd thought he'd retained some of the edge from the old days, but apparently not. His little brother and sweet, innocent-looking Laura could be pulling a drug-smuggling operation right under his nose.

Jaw clenched, Nick covered the distance to the rest room in a few quick strides and shoved open the door. There she was, perched on the vanity. She looked up and saw him, her eyes round and her mouth open, as if she thought he'd gone crazy. He was beginning to wonder the same thing. He forced a grin. "Whoops. Wrong door," he said, and backed out again.

4

LAURA DIDN'T RECOVER for a full ten seconds. She'd never had a man barge in on her in the women's room before. Nick had caught her sitting and thinking about . . . him. The more she considered the look of determination on his face, the more convinced she was that he hadn't made a mistake. He'd meant to check up on her. Then, when he'd seen she was okay, he'd made up the first excuse that came to mind.

Laura picked up her purse and went into the hall. He wasn't there. Probably hanging around in the men's room to make his excuse seem plausible, she thought, returning to the table. Neither of them had eaten much of their meal, but she wasn't hungry anymore. She sipped her iced tea and waited.

When Nick slid into the booth, she pushed her plate aside and folded her hands on the table. "I don't believe you came into that rest room by accident, Nick Hooper."

He looked guilty. "You're right."

"You came to check on me, because I was in there so long, didn't you?"

"Yes."

"I'm flattered that you're so concerned about me."

Nick pushed his plate aside, too. Obviously the meal was over for both of them. "Listen, Laura. You might as well know I tried to call Lance in Seattle. The seminar director told me Lance had canceled out at the last minute. He's not there."

"Not there?" Laura was confused. "I thought you said it was important to his career."

"Maybe something came up that was more important."

Laura had a chilling thought. Lance could have found out about the stalled car and decided to come to Monterey. Instead of having to deal with him eventually, she'd have to confront him now and tell him her feelings had changed, that she was interested in his brother. "Did you try him at home?"

"Yes. I got the machine and there were no messages from Lance."

Laura voiced her unwelcome thought. "Maybe he's on his way down here. Maybe he talked to Atkins and knows there's a problem."

"That's possible." He studied her, his gray eyes thoughtful. "But he seemed so intent on that seminar."

"He could be concerned about me, I guess. Although, to be honest, canceling that seminar and charging down here to the rescue doesn't sound like Lance."

"So where is he?"

"Don't ask me."

"You're the logical person to ask," Nick persisted.

She was becoming irritated. "You act as if there's something I'm not telling you."

"Is there?"

"No." Her response was clipped. "I know only what you've told me, that he had a last-minute chance to attend a seminar that was important to his career. Now he's canceled it, but he's not at home, either. That's the extent of my information, Nick. Sorry."

He looked at her for a moment longer, as if waiting for something.

"What? What is it?"

"Nothing." He signaled for the check. "Let's go back to the room. I need to call my client about tomorrow, and I can try a few of Lance's friends to find out if any of them know where he is."

"Are you worried?"

"If you mean do I think something's happened to him, no, I'm not worried about that. He called to cancel the seminar, so he wasn't in an accident or anything. Besides, he carries plenty of identification. If anything had happened to him, there'd be a message on the machine from the authorities. Whatever he's up to, he's not anxious for me to know about it, or he'd have left me a message. He could have done that when he canceled the seminar trip."

"Well, I wish I could help you, but I can't imagine what he's doing," Laura said, wanting to distance herself from Lance's odd behavior. "The whole thing's pretty strange."

"Yes, isn't it?"

Nick paid the bill, and Laura decided Lance's disappearing act was further evidence that he wasn't the man for her. She'd been upset that he'd booked the seminar in the first place. Canceling it at the last minute seemed even more irresponsible. Nick wouldn't behave like that; he'd already proven she could count on him when the chips were down. He'd even braved the women's room to satisfy himself that she was safe, charging through the door, ready to do battle if she'd needed him. But now he thought she was withholding information about Lance, even scheming with him. She was hurt. Nick should have realized she was more straightforward than that.

They walked back to the hotel in uncomfortable silence. Evening fog dampened Laura's face and circled the street lamps with eerie halos. This business about Lance's disappearance had spoiled their cozy alliance.

They climbed the outside stairs to the second floor, the wooden steps creaking as they went. Nick inserted the key into the lock and swung the door open. Suddenly all Laura could see was the king-size bed taking up the major portion of the room. She stepped inside. She had no idea what to do next.

"TV?" he asked, tossing the room key into an ashtray. "I'm going to make my call." He gestured toward the phone on the bedside table.

Laura sized up the situation. The room was set up to watch television from the bed. "I'm not much for TV," she said. "Maybe I'll brush my teeth." She had to walk past Nick to retrieve her overnight bag. The room was growing progressively smaller. "Excuse me."

He moved back slightly to let her go by. She picked up the bag and started back, not looking at him, yet she sensed his warmth and caught his musky scent. It would be so easy to put down the bag, hold out her arms and lift her lips for another heated kiss. Perhaps then he'd know she was sincere. She hesitated.

"I'd better call Joanne," he said, his voice low.

"Joanne?" She glanced up at him in confusion.

"My client."

"Oh. Of course. I'll...I'll brush my teeth." She went quickly into the bathroom and closed the door. When she emerged, Nick was still on the phone. Laura picked up a tourist magazine from the table and sat down in the armchair beside it. She hated to eavesdrop but couldn't avoid it.

Nick sat hunched on the edge of the bed, and sounded angry. "No, I didn't realize you knew Mr. Chambers. Perhaps you should have listened to him when he warned you I'd be unreliable.... That's your prerogative, Joanne. I'm sorry if you counted on my being there tomorrow, but this is an emergency. I hope to be there the day after that, but I can't even promise I'll... All right, we'll leave it that way. Do what you feel you have to. Goodbye." Nick hung up and cursed.

Laura put down the magazine. "Why don't you drive back tonight, Nick? I couldn't help overhearing that, and it sounds as if you'll lose some business. I'll be fine here."

"No." He tunneled his fingers through his hair. "There's no winning that one, anyway. I've been nervous about it, even before I knew the stakes."

"What stakes?"

Nick sighed and flopped onto the bed. "Joanne is an unhappy lady with lots of money and a husband who ignores her." He closed his eyes. "She told me the other day that she'd interviewed six carpenters before she hired me for the job. I know some of them—genuine craftsmen and happily married. I don't think she picked me because I'm handy with a hammer."

"Oh."

"From the tone of her voice when I said I wouldn't be there tomorrow, I think she had a little surprise planned for me. She's been working up to it for days, wearing skimpy outfits, tossing out suggestive remarks, leaning over my shoulder when I'm working."

A warm flush spread over Laura's skin as she stared at Nick lying on the bed. The buttons on his denim shirt strained a little across his muscled chest, and the faded softness of his jeans wrapped around powerful thighs. Between those thighs, she had no trouble imagining . . . A wave of desire flowed through her. She understood Joanne's behavior. "I suppose that would be an awkward situation," she managed.

"I didn't even know how awkward." He opened his eyes and looked up at the ceiling. "Apparently she and her husband socialize with P. Delwood Chambers and his wife. They came over to the house, saw my work in progress and asked who was doing it. Old P. Delwood is just looking for more reasons to blackball me. Joanne's threatening to give them to him."

"What could happen? You have your own business, don't you?"

"Yes, but you see, I want something." He rolled onto his stomach and propped his chin up on his hands to look at her. "I've been trying for the past year to get a contractor's license. That's my dream, Laura. P. Delwood Chambers is an important man in California, and he's seen to it that my application hits one snag after another."

She wondered if Nick had any idea how appealing he looked with his tousled hair and intent expression. "What has this Chambers guy got against you?" she asked.

"I stole his car."

"Nick!"

His mouth curved into a wry smile. "I told you I used to be a juvenile delinquent."

"Oh, you mean you stole his car fifteen years ago." She relaxed. "That's different. I thought you meant you took it last week or something."

"I might as well have, the way he acts. That all happened down in L.A., where I grew up. I moved to the Bay Area partly to get away from my old reputation. Unfortunately, P. Delwood moved here, too, and somehow got wind of my license application. He has friends in the bureaucracy, so he's informed them I'm not to be trusted and I sure as hell shouldn't be bonded. He told Joanne, too. Now I know why she kept talking about tattoos and how sexy she thought they were. Chambers must have told her I had one."

"You do?" Laura was still trying to assimilate the two Nicks; the one she saw before her and the hell-raiser he'd described in the restaurant.

"Unfortunately." He rolled onto his back and sat up. "I've looked into having it removed, but it's not a fun thing to do, so I've left it."

"I've never known anybody who had a tattoo."

"You have been sheltered." He started unbuttoning his shirt. "Here, I'll show you—"

"That's okay." Laura's pulse was racing enough without having Nick take off his shirt. She'd bet he had a sprinkling of hair on his chest, a flat stomach.... "I think I'll . . . get some ice." She jumped up, rummaged in her purse for change and grabbed the ice bucket. "We could use something cold to drink, couldn't we? I'll get something from the machine."

"If you say so." He smiled. "Laura, you don't have to be afraid of me. Even in my worst days, I've always been kind to women, children and animals."

"Oh, it's not that. It's . . . Let me get that ice. I'll be right back."

"I'll be here."

Yes, he certainly would, Laura thought as she raced out the door and down the stairs. He'd be there all through the blessed night. She should decide what she wanted to do. Decide now, before she went back inside. She wasn't terribly experienced with men. There'd been her steady in high school, a fumbling boy who'd ended up marrying one of her friends a year after they graduated. Now he worked on his parents' peanut farm. Laura hadn't become sexually involved with anyone else until Lance had shown up.

Laura hadn't realized just how tame her feelings for Lance had been until today, when she'd reacted with such force to Nick. She'd even wondered if she was one of those women who lacked the seething passion she'd read about in novels. Lance was good-looking, and she'd tried to imagine herself madly in love with him. Her coworkers had thought she should be. Now that she knew what real desire felt like, she wouldn't be able to fool herself about Lance anymore.

The ice machine was at the foot of the stairs, inside an alcove. She placed the bucket under the spout and pushed the button. Ice rattled into the plastic container, blocking out any sounds around her. Suddenly Nick sprinted past her into the parking lot. She jumped, releasing the button.

"Get up to the room and lock the door!" he called over his shoulder.

Her heart thudded in her chest. She clutched the bucket and peered into the darkness after him. He rounded the corner and was gone, leaving her feeling suddenly vulnerable. Ice clattered out of the bucket and spilled onto the steps as she ran toward the room. Careening inside the door, she closed it and turned the dead bolt. Then she checked the bathroom, the closet and under the bed, to make sure no one had gotten into the room ahead of her. She was alone. Panting, still holding the ice bucket, she slumped onto the bed.

A soft tap came at the door. "Laura, it's Nick. I lost the guy."

She got up and let him in.

He was breathing hard, and sweat dampened his face and the front of his shirt. "I should have gone with you," he said, locking the door behind him. "I knew it as soon as you'd been gone twenty seconds. I flew out that door, and that's when I saw him."

"The chubby guy." Laura walked to the table and set down the ice bucket. Her hands were shaking. The blinds were open, so she closed them. "I've heard about men like him who get fixated on a woman, but I can't understand it. He followed me all the way up here. He knows exactly where we're staying. What's wrong with him? Why would he behave like that?"

Behind her, Nick was silent.

"It's not fair," she said. Tears of frustration gathered in her eyes. "Other women strike out on their own and don't have cars break down and psychos follow them and their boyfriends disappear. Why does it have to happen to me, the very first time I—? Oh, damn!" She pressed her fingers to her eyes, trying unsuccessfully to stem the rush of tears.

"Take it easy." Nick put his hands upon her shoulders and turned her to face him. "You'll get past this."

His features looked blurred through her tears, his gray eyes soft as evening clouds. "You're the only good thing about this trip so far," she said, hearing her voice thicken with emotion. "You and the ocean."

"That puts me in good company." He smiled.

"Nick . . . please kiss me again."

He caught his breath. "We don't need to fool anyone now, Laura."

She looked at him steadily. "Not even ourselves."

"I don't think I ever did fool myself, Laura. I've always known what I wanted. But are you sure?"

"Yes." She lifted her lips. They were moist with tears. Slowly, tenderly, he kissed them away. A sweet ache began throbbing deep within her.

"You taste like the ocean," he whispered, gathering her into his arms.

This time she knew what to expect, and he didn't disappoint her. His warm mouth moved gently, coaxing a response that had simmered beneath the surface since their first kiss. In the space of a sigh she invited his tongue inside, opened herself to the intimate caress that hinted at what would follow. He moaned, and she pressed herself against him, so tightly that she could feel his heart's wild beating.

He kissed her until they were breathless. He moved his lips from her mouth to her cheek, to the soft lobe of her ear. "I want you so much," he murmured. His hands slid up the small of her back under her sweatshirt and knit polo. "I want you and I shouldn't. Not yet."

She arched against him. "We didn't plan this, Nick. It's not your fault there was only one room. And the way we both feel . . ."

"How do you know I didn't plan it?" He kissed the curve of her neck and unfastened her bra.

"Did you?" She almost wished he had; it would be evidence of his longing for her.

"Not this. Not like this," he said, reclaiming her lips as he cradled the fullness of her breast.

Dizzying sensations swirled through Laura's body. So this was what all the songs, the poems, the stories were about. She kissed him feverishly; would time run out before she could get enough of him?

"You have to trust me," he whispered against her mouth.

"I trust you."

With a groan he kissed her again, deeper, thrusting his tongue into her mouth. She writhed against him, wanting to somehow become him. She'd never experienced such a drive for unity, for completion. He stripped her sweatshirt, polo and bra over her head in one practiced motion. She welcomed the freedom and relished the glow in his eyes, his smile when he looked at her uncovered breasts.

They were only steps from the bed. Without being quite sure how they got there, Laura found herself stretched beneath Nick on the wide mattress. When his mouth captured her breast, she gasped with pleasure at the slight friction of his beard.

He rolled onto his back, taking her with him. She abandoned herself to him, allowing him to stroke and knead and caress her body, remove her clothing, drive her insane with the touch of his hands and lips. She would give him anything. Anything.

Vaguely she realized that he'd unbuttoned his shirt, and she leaned forward to kiss his bare skin. Soft, curly hair tickled her lips and nose. Her breasts grazed his body, and as she flicked her tongue over his nipples, he shuddered.

"Take the rest . . . off," he said, his voice hoarse.

A surge of heat poured through her. She knew she was moist and ready for him. She trembled so that she fumbled the job of taking off his jeans and underwear, but once they were gone, she closed her fingers around him and heard him moan her name. Now it was her turn to take command. She loved knowing she was driving him wild in the same way he'd affected her.

She caressed him until he gripped her shoulders and urged her to lie on her back. His gaze found hers, then he moved over her.

"Yes," she whispered, opening to him.

He came to her then, thrusting forward, burying himself with a sureness that nearly sent her over the edge. He paused, as if to prolong her pleasure and his. Then, with exquisitely timed movements he pushed her closer and closer; he seemed to feel what she felt, to breathe when she breathed. She'd never been loved like this.

He gasped and drove deeper. That was all she needed. Their release came in unison, a climax so powerful that Laura lost all sense of herself as a separate person. Her only reality was the pulsing desire that had made them one. Her spinning world gradually slowed, she relaxed the arms that held him tight, and realized that no matter what happened, even if Nick wasn't destined to be in her future, at least she'd had this—something shc'd doubted the existence of, something she would spend the rest of her life cherishing . . . and searching for.

Nick sighed and nestled his head in the curve of her shoulder. She felt his heartbeat slow. She stroked his back and the nape of his neck.

"I feel as if I should say something to you," he murmured, "but words seem so inadequate."

"I know."

"We both thought it could be like this."

"Yes."

"Now we know."

"I'm glad this happened, Nick. No matter what."

"Good. So am I." He kissed the curve of her throat. "But we were pretty hasty, Laura. I always use protection, except this time. I allowed myself to assume that because of Lance, you—"

"I take birth control pills," she interrupted softly, "but it's no longer because of Lance, is it?"

"No." He traced the outline of her lips with a gentle finger. "Everything's changed." He was silent for a moment. "I fixed the window, Laura."

"The window? You mean so nobody could get in the room?"

"Not this window, the one in the Cadillac. I fixed it while you were making your calls at the restaurant at Big Sur."

"Oh." She couldn't imagine why he'd tell her something like that now, but she admitted to not knowing everything about the way the male mind worked. "Well, that will save Atkins some time. He told me not to worry about it, that it had been broken since he bought the car and he'd get the thing fixed in San Francisco. Now I guess he doesn't have to."

Nick propped his cheek upon his palm and looked at her. He studied her carefully and finally smiled. "You're either a fantastic liar, or you really don't know what's going on. I'd bet everything I own that you don't know what's going on, and that makes me very happy."

She narrowed her eyes. "What on earth are you talking about? First you rave on about fixing windows, and now you accuse me of not knowing what's happening.

You're not making any sense, and I wonder if I've just been insulted."

"Just the opposite. In this case, not knowing anything is good, because it means you're innocent."

"Wait a minute. Inexperienced, yes, but innocent?"

He laughed. "Listen to me, you wonderful and decidedly not-so-innocent woman. There was a reason the window wouldn't close. There was a package wedged into the door, behind the door panel. I took it out and hid it in the air vent of my truck."

She stared at him as the impact of what he'd said sank in. "Oh, my God!"

"We can assume, if Atkins told you not to bother with the broken window, that he's using this little run of yours for smuggling."

Laura felt cold. "Smuggling what?"

"I don't know. Didn't have time to unwrap the package. Maybe drugs."

"And you thought I knew about it?" Laura shuddered at the horror of knowing she might have been carrying drugs, that Nick now had the package in his truck. "You made love to me and everything, thinking I was a drug smuggler? Are you so blasé about things like that?"

His expression darkened. "No. I've done some illegal things in my life, but I'd cut off my right arm before I'd run drugs." He gazed at her. "Which may give you some idea of how much I wanted you. Making love to you was all I could think about, no matter what you were involved in, even drugs, which I hate with a passion. Besides, if you had known about the stash, I was planning to reform you, make you go straight. Didn't you hear all those things I said about commitments that don't count?"

"I thought you were talking about Lance and me," she whispered.

"Not exactly, although I don't think you owe anything to a guy that's foolish enough to put you in this kind of danger. Commitments should go both ways. He may be my brother, but he's screwed up this little business, but good."

"But he didn't know! Atkins was just a customer at the bank. Lance couldn't have known about the smuggling."

Nick combed a strand of hair back from her cheek. "Are you sure?"

"Nick, what are you thinking? He's your brother!"

"He's also mysteriously disappeared."

"I'm sure there's a good explanation. Maybe you should call your house again. He's probably there right now, nursing a case of the flu."

"Let's hope." He leaned down and kissed her gently. "Don't go away."

"No chance."

He smiled and levered himself up. Swinging his feet to the floor, he reached for the telephone. As he punched in the number, Laura caressed the broad expanse of his back. He turned, and tucking a hand around her waist, scooted her closer. The movement flexed his biceps, and it was then that Laura noticed the tattoo.

A coiled snake, fangs bared, crept over the inscription Vipers. She stared in fascination at the tattoo, which rippled as Nick absently stroked her hip.

She could tell he was retrieving messages. Then he left a second one for Lance, telling him to call Monterey the minute he got in. Lance was still missing. An air of unreality crept over Laura. The man she'd once planned to marry might be involved in a drug-smuggling scheme, and she'd just made wonderful love with his brother, who bore the mark of a gang who called themselves the Vipers. "I don't think we're in New Mexico anymore, Toto," she murmured.

5

LANCE HOOPER had never scaled a seven-foot fence topped with razor wire or faced two snarling Dobermans. A life devoted to tennis matches, fraternity parties and air-conditioned offices hadn't prepared him for breaking into a wrecking yard. The only thing he feared more than climbing the fence and meeting the dogs was not doing it. He'd discovered that Atkins was stupid, but had seen enough true crime movies and news reports to know that stupidity had never stopped people from committing acts of violence.

He crouched in the dark, several yards away from the fence. He spotted the Cadillac in the yard's floodlights and took note of the dogs and the razor wire, then left to pick up supplies. Atkins had been right. Benny would never have made it into the yard, or if he had, he wouldn't have made it out again. It took more than athletic ability to do this; it took some brains. Benny was even dumber than Atkins, but somehow those two imbeciles had stumbled upon a plan that promised to pay big bucks. Lance wasn't about to pass that up, no matter how stupid his partners were.

Soon he was back. On the passenger seat of his red Toyota sat a package of hamburger laced with mild sleeping pills. Tied along one side of the car was a ten-foot length of PVC pipe he'd found at a construction site.

The cyclone fence wasn't in perfect repair. He lured the growling dogs to a hole big enough to toss the doctored meat through. They fought over the chunks, and one seemed to get more than the other, but eventually both walked unsteadily to a trailer and curled up beside the steps.

Lance waited a good fifteen minutes more, to be sure the dogs were asleep. Then he untied the pipe. He hadn't been a track superstar in college, but he'd been pretty good at pole-vaulting. If the pipe didn't break, he'd get over without touching the razor wire. On the opposite side was a big pile of old tires that he could land on. He made a couple of practice runs to get the feel of the distance with the pole in his hand. The running felt good. He didn't shake so much now.

Checking to make sure the screwdriver was still in his back pocket, he took a deep breath and started to run. At the critical moment he shoved the end of the pipe into the dirt and pushed off. As he sailed through the air, his pants leg caught on something sharp, and the material ripped all the way to his crotch. He fell onto the tires, and they weren't as soft as they'd looked. He banged his head and one arm on metal rims that had been left on some of the tires.

He rolled off the pile and staggered to his feet. The screwdriver had fallen out of his pocket, so he had to dig through the tires until he found it. His head ached, his arm ached, his pants were ruined, and his good white shirt was covered with black smudges, but he hadn't broken anything as far as he could tell, and the dogs hadn't stirred. Wiping his hands on his torn pants, he headed for the Cadillac.

He pulled out the key Atkins had given him and was soon inside the car, taking off the door panel. His shaking problem returned when he realized he hadn't gone past this point in his planning. Although he could shove the mask out the hole he'd used to get the meat in, he had no pole on this side to help him vault back.

The panel came free and he looked inside. Then he looked again in horrified disbelief. The supports were there, the way Atkins had said they would be, but the space was empty. Lance felt sick to his stomach. Atkins wouldn't believe the mask was gone. He'd be sure Lance was trying to double-cross him.

Lance fought his panic and tried to think. Laura and Nick might have it, but maybe not. He couldn't go to them and risk giving himself away. The towing people could have found it, or maybe Benny had somehow managed to snatch it before the car was locked in the yard.

Locked in. He had to get out of there. Now. He replaced the door panel and locked the car. He couldn't climb over the fence. The razor wire would rip him to shreds. He walked around the perimeter until he came to the hole where he'd tossed the hamburger in. It was less than a foot wide. He'd have to enlarge it somehow.

He found a cinder block and began banging away at the ragged edges of the hole. His arms ached from the effort and he could smell his own sweat. Finally the hole seemed large enough to wriggle through. Dropping to his hands and knees, he pushed his head and shoulders through, wincing when the ragged edges of the wire tore at his shirt, just scraping his chest. Then he heard a dog growl.

He looked over his shoulder. A Doberman was poised, haunches bunched and fangs glistening in the wrecking yard lights. Frantically scrabbling with his hands at the dirt on the other side, Lance managed to get all but one leg through the fence before the dog lunged. Teeth sank into his calf, but he wriggled and pulled with such desperation that he wrenched himself loose from the dog's powerful jaws.

His leg burned with pain; he scrambled to his feet and half limped, half ran toward the car. If he could get through the hole, so could the Doberman. He glanced back to see how close the dog was, but instead of snapping at his heels, the animal was pacing the fence line, snarling and whining. It had been trained not to leave the yard. He was free.

He ran to the car, got in and locked all the doors. Then he sat there, bruised and scraped and bleeding, and wondered where the hell to go. Somewhere where Atkins wouldn't find him. No way was he going to stick around to take the rap. San Francisco was a big city. With luck, maybe he could lose himself there until the mask turned up. Someone had it—the wrong some-one—and Lance didn't envy them one bit.

LAURA WATCHED Nick's expression harden; he pushed the disconnect button and dialed a different number. She traced the coiled snake with her finger and saw him glance at her and frown when he noticed what she was doing. Then someone answered at the other end of the line, and he turned his attention to the telephone.

"Yeah, Sherry? Sorry to bother you so late, but is Lance there? Yes, he was supposed to be, but he canceled, and he's not at home, so I thought . . . Okay . . . Yeah, if you hear from him. I'm in Monterey. Here's the number. Reverse the charges. Right. Thanks, Sherry." He hung up and looked at Laura. "Maybe I will have it removed."

She covered his arm with her hand, as if to protect his skin. "Don't ever do that. I've heard it hurts a lot. I wouldn't want you to—"

"It wasn't the pain. It was the expense, and the possibility they couldn't remove it without massive scarring, which would look worse."

"I don't mind, Nick. It doesn't bother me."

"Liar." He turned and placed his palms on either side of her head. "I saw the look on your face," he said, leaning forward to nuzzle her lips.

"It's just so hard to think of you that way—fighting, zooming around on motorcycles, acting wild, when you're really so gentle."

He lifted his head and gazed at her. "I'm not always gentle, Laura."

She remembered his grim expression when he'd barged into the rest room after her, his scowl when he hadn't been able to reach Lance. "With me, then."

"Always with you." He kissed her forehead. "Always."

"Nick, you don't get into fights now, do you?"

"No. Although at the moment I feel like beating the tar out of my little brother."

Mention of Lance reminded her of Nick's last call. "Who's Sherry?"

Nick met her questioning glance steadily. "Someone at Lance's bank."

"But you thought she might be over there tonight. That sounds like more than a mere coworker."

"Yeah."

When Nick didn't elaborate, Laura filled in the blanks. In the six months she'd been refusing dates and staying home, Lance had not. All those candlelit dinners back in Clovis, all those pretty words Lance had said to her, meant nothing to him. Lance had been using her. The knowledge hurt, but it also eased her feelings of guilt about making love with Nick.

"Jealous?"

Laura shook her head. What she'd experienced with Lance was infatuation. If it had been love, she would have been more than jealous. She would have been heartbroken.

"He's not right for you. I've suspected that for a long time, but I was worried about him. Now I don't want *you* to make any mistakes."

She reached up and stroked his bristly chin. "No danger of that anymore, Nick."

"I should have shaved. You're rubbed all pink."

"I loved it."

"So did I. In fact . . ."

She pressed her fingers to his lips and stopped him from kissing her again. "Shouldn't we get that thing, whatever it is, out of the truck?"

He caught her fingertips and kissed them. "I don't think anybody knows it's in there. In an open parking lot someone, especially that pudgy guy, might see us. Then we could be in for it."

"Should we go to the police?"

"If you want to, we will, but I'd like to track Lance down first. If he's in on this, I want to get to him before the police do. Maybe there's some way to get him out of it with minimal trouble."

"I thought you wanted to beat the tar out of him?"

"I do, but I'd also like to save him from himself. He's being a stupid jerk, but having a record is no fun. I ought to know."

Laura respected Nick's tolerance. She didn't feel the same allegiance to Lance, but if Nick wanted to stop his baby brother breaking the law, she'd go along. "Lance is lucky to have you in his corner, Nick."

He gave her a wry smile. "As I said on the phone, what are big brothers for?"

Laura absorbed the magnetic pull of that lopsided smile, her heart swelling with an emotion that had a little to do with lust, with what they'd shared here in this bed. But a more powerful feeling tugged at her, too. Nick's nobility and courage were evident. It wouldn't take much to make her fall in love with him.

"What's that look for?" he asked.

She couldn't tell him . . . not yet, at least. "I was just thinking that I'm glad you're here."

"You mean in Monterey, in this room, or in this bed?"

"All of the above." She pulled him down for a kiss that soon turned into more. She'd wondered if the wild sense of abandon she'd felt the first time would be a unique experience, but as he began to touch her, she realized that breathlessness and dizziness would be normal whenever she was being loved by Nick Hooper.

THE PHONE on the bedside table rang at six the next morning. Nick answered it while Laura struggled out of a dream. She was being chased, but the person chasing her kept changing from Lance to Atkins, and finally to the pudgy man from the restaurant. She sat up in bed and rubbed her eyes, forcing the dream into the background. Nick was here, she told herself. Nick wouldn't let anything happen to her.

He was talking in a low voice.

"Is it Lance?" she whispered, touching his shoulder.

He shook his head. "Okay. We'll be down right away." He hung up and turned to her. "The Cadillac's been stolen from the wrecking yard."

She stared at him. "Somebody was after the package?"

"I think so." He reached for the phone again. "Let me try Lance."

"You don't think he could have stolen it?"

"No." He punched in the number. "Whoever it was knocked down the fence with some heavy equipment. The police think they took the car away on a flatbed."

"You don't think Lance could have done that, if he was desperate?"

Nick shook his head and covered the mouthpiece with his hand. "I don't think Lance has ever driven a pickup truck, let alone something powerful enough to bulldoze fences and haul away Cadillacs. Besides, there was something else. Whoever it was shot the guard dogs."

Laura winced. "You're right. He wouldn't do something like that." Fear seeped like a poisonous gas into her mind. "Do you think it was Atkins? I can believe that of him, unfortunately."

"Maybe." Nick dropped the receiver into its cradle. "Lance isn't home. He hasn't been there or taken the messages off the machine. What in hell is he up to?"

Laura tried to stay calm. "What about the police? Should we tell them about the package?" She didn't want to sound like a coward, yet she heard the note of anxiety in her voice.

Nick must have heard it, too. He stroked her hair. "Do you want to?"

She considered the possibilities. The more time that went by with no word from Lance, the more she feared Lance was mixed up in the smuggling. If she and Nick surrendered the package before they found Lance, the police would have enough information to hunt Lance down, along with anyone else involved. Lance had been a good friend to her, and without him she wouldn't have made the move to California so soon. Apparently he'd done something stupid, but maybe she and Nick could convince him to turn himself in along with the smuggled package, so that he might not be punished so severely.

"No, let's not tell the police yet. We need to find Lance first, if we possibly can."

"Okay," he said slowly, "but I've decided to take the 'we' out of this, Laura. After we talk to the police about the Cadillac, I'll rent you a car so you can drive back to Clovis. I don't mind dealing with Lance's mess, but the party's getting rough. You shouldn't be exposed to this kind of danger."

"What?"

He took her by the shoulders. "Whoever stole the car is capable of killing dogs. They have guns, and they may be capable of killing people, too, for all I know. You're an innocent bystander in all this."

"So are you!"

"Not anymore. I transferred that stuff to my truck. I'm already concealing things from the authorities, but I'm willing to take that risk. You've never been in this kind of trouble before. I have. I also have a general idea of how to handle it. It's time for you to go home, Laura."

"Of all the nerve!" She twisted away from him. "If that wasn't a pat on the head I've never felt one!"

"Now don't get me wrong. I think you're wonderful and brave and—"

"And a sheltered little hick who can't deal with the big, bad world. Well, I may have been sheltered, and I may be a hick, but I'm a fast learner and I intend to handle whatever comes my way."

"I just want to keep you safe," he pleaded.

"Well, you can't. No one can keep anyone safe. I may not know much, but I know that." She lifted her chin.

"I want respect, Nick, not patronage. When you made love to me you didn't treat me like a china doll, so don't start now. I'm a grown woman. I've chosen to change my life, and I'm not about to let some macho carpenter, some former gang member, change it back for me. I am not, I repeat, *not* going back to New Mexico. Got that?"

He gazed at her. Slowly a smile curved his lips. "Maybe I underestimated you."

"See that it doesn't happen again. We're in this together, mister, like it or not."

He glanced over her unclothed body. "I think I'm going to like it."

"I wasn't referring to that."

"I know." He paused. "But I should have realized that you wouldn't run home just because I suggested it. When you make love, you give it everything you have. I should have known you'd be that way about other things, too."

She started to tell him that she'd never made love that way in her life, that he'd been the magic element that had created such abandonment. But she had no idea where the two of them were heading. A moment ago he'd been ready to send her away without so much as a whisper of a future. She couldn't say what was in her heart. Not yet.

Nick smiled and reached out to rub his thumb across her lower lip. "I wish to hell we were here under different circumstances," he said.

"Me, too."

"Maybe you'd better hit the shower before I forget all about our noble plans. I'll make a few more calls, see if I can stir up any news of our boy Lance."

"Okay." She slid to the edge of the mattress next to him and swung her feet to the floor.

"One more thing."

"Yes?"

"This." He crushed her to him and plundered her mouth. When he released her, she was gasping. "Now go, woman."

She stood, although she doubted that her knees would support her. She picked up her overnight bag from the floor.

"You're really something, Laura Rhodes," Nick said softly.

She turned and smiled when she saw the rapt expression on his face. "You, too," she murmured. She started into the bathroom, then paused. "I just remembered. All my stuff, except a change of clothes in here and my overnight gear, was in that car. I'm wiped out." As she spoke, she realized she didn't really care. Not after a kiss like that. Everything she had dragged to California really belonged to her New Mexico life, anyway. She could have traveled much lighter.

"I can't promise you'll get your stuff back, either. Sure you want to stay? California hasn't been very good to you so far."

Laura ran the tip of her tongue slowly over her lips. "No, but you have!"

His gray eyes darkened and he gripped the edge of the bed. "You'd better get in there."

With a teasing sway of her hips she turned and stepped inside the bathroom. She'd never experienced her own sexual power before and it was a heady feeling. She couldn't go back to New Mexico, to her old life there. She wouldn't begin to fit in.

NICK GAVE HIMSELF a moment to recover before he began searching his memory for the phone numbers he needed. He hadn't expected ever to use them again, and he wouldn't now if it weren't for Laura. But he could use some backup, and knew two guys who had once promised to be there anytime, anyplace, if he needed them. He needed them now.

That wasn't all he needed, though. The shower was running in the bathroom, and she'd left the door open. He dialed the first number, closed his eyes and pictured her in there under the spray. Instantly he grew hard and almost hung up, but a man answered, a voice he remembered from a distant past.

"Hey, Banjo," he said, forcing his mind away from Laura.

"Hey, Hammer," the man replied.

Nick smiled. Trust Banjo to act cool, as if they'd last spoken yesterday instead of fourteen years ago. "I need a favor."

"You got it."

"I have to drive the road from Monterey to San Francisco with some tender merchandise in my truck. I could use a discreet escort."

"I'm there."

"Any chance you could get Deadline?"

"Yep. When?"

Nick glanced at the digital clock built into the television set. "I'll stall until noon, to give you time. Look for a white truck that says Hooper Carpentry on the side. You'll recognize the license plate."

"Want us to hang around in 'Frisco?"

"Might be good for a day or two. You can stay at my place if—"

"Nope. You don't need that, Hammer. You're straight now. We'll be around, that's all. Give us your phone number so we can check in. That's enough."

Nick gave him his home number. "And thanks, buddy."

"No problem."

Nick hung up. Just like that, as if nothing had changed. Maybe for Banjo and Deadline, nothing had. He stood and glanced in the direction of the bathroom. The shower was still on, and Laura was humming. He'd told the guy at the wrecking yard they'd be right down, but he'd just promised Banjo he'd stall the trip until noon. Checkout was eleven. Once they left here, they probably wouldn't be back. Now that he had a plan for getting Laura and the truck home safely, he had a little time on his hands.

He walked into the bathroom and pulled the shower curtain aside. She stopped humming and turned to look at him. Her hair, glossy as a raven's wing, was slicked back from her forehead, making her look innocent and sexy at the same time. Water collected in droplets on her eyelashes and ran in rivulets over her breasts. Her nipples were large and pale from the warmth of the shower, but as he watched they darkened and drew into firm nubs. He glanced into her eyes. Her eyes were not innocent. They smoldered with the same fire that was licking at him.

"You're getting water all over the floor," she said, her voice husky.

He stepped into the tub and slid his hand beneath the wet curtain of her hair. He stroked upward from the nape of her neck, cradling her head to savor her moist lips. He moved slowly, watching her eyelids close, her lips part as he came near. She smelled of shampoo and coconut. With his other hand he massaged the small of her back, his palm against her water-slick skin. He had to restrain himself; he wanted her so much, his whole body shook.

He moved closer and the shower spray pinged against his face. She draped her damp arms over his shoulders and leaned into the kiss, brushing her nipples against his chest. Her hands moved over his back and buttocks, finger-painting her desire.

He longed to take her again, but first...first he would cover every inch of her body with his mouth and tongue. He couldn't explain why she affected him like this, and had ever since their first kiss. The night before, he'd been willing to excuse her for breaking the law; nothing had been more important than making love to this woman. Reason deserted him every time he touched her, something that had never happened to him before.

Her body lured him, her caress turned him into a breathless supplicant. He left the warm haven of her mouth and pressed his lips against the hollow of her throat. He licked the moisture gathered there.

"You're getting wet," she whispered as spray dampened his hair.

"That's what showers are for."

"And for this?" She rotated her hips against his and nudged his burgeoning desire.

"Absolutely for this." Cradling her in his arms, he kissed his way down the slope of one breast and captured the prize waiting at the tip. He loved her quick little gasp of delight and drew her into his mouth; her breathing quickened as he curled his tongue around her nipple.

He tried not to roughen her skin with his beard, but she grasped his head and urged him closer. "Don't baby me," she murmured.

"All right." He cupped her other breast and took that nipple into his mouth. She moaned and buried her fingers in his hair while he kneaded her plump breasts and savored the pebbled texture of her nipple against his tongue.

A blanket of warm steam wrapped itself around him, coaxing him to submerge himself in the delights she offered. His groin pulsed, but he wanted this first, this complete knowing. At last he was on his knees, his tongue probing first her navel, then lower to the sweet secrets of her femininity. Water splashed around them and muted her soft cries.

She clutched his shoulders and her legs trembled. He supported her, hands spread over the firm mounds of her bottom, and loved her relentlessly. At last she dug her fingers into his shoulder muscles and cried out as spasms rocked her. Nearly bursting himself, he rose, still holding her tight. He eased her against the tiled wall of the stall.

The spray hit his buttocks until he entered her and moved out of range of the water. He'd never known a woman to be so open, so soft and yet so tight around him. She kissed him frantically, pulling him against her. He eased out again, felt the water pelt like tiny needles, urging him back inside her body. Then he erupted with a force that made him gasp. Yet he knew, no matter how complete his release, that it wouldn't be long before he'd need her again. She was good, good for him, with him. Almost . . . He pushed the thought away, but it came back. . . . Almost too good to be true.

6

IT WAS NEARLY TEN before they checked out of the hotel. Laura had given up trying to hurry Nick along. After making love in the shower, they'd dried each other off and Nick had borrowed her razor in order to shave. She'd begun to dress when he appeared from the bathroom, freshly shaved, and had begun systematically removing the clothes she'd put on. She'd never met a man so insatiable, but what still astonished her was her own hunger. All he had to do was touch her and she wanted him again. Finally, after a second shower, they'd left the room.

"Let me take care of the bill," Laura said as they walked down the stairs. "You've paid for a drink and dinner, and gas to come down here and drive back. If you don't let me handle some of the extra expenses, I'll have trouble maintaining my feeling of independence."

He glanced at her. "Wouldn't want that."

"So I can pay?"

"If you want to, Laura."

"I do. I'll walk over to the office. You can meet me outside the door with the truck."

"Don't talk to strangers."

"Same goes for you," she shot back and walked away.

The morning fog had burned off, leaving a sky so bright she fished in her purse for her sunglasses. Stray drops of morning dew sparkled on the rose petals in the garden. Laura took a deep sniff of the fragrant air. She felt like whistling, something that could be considered strange behavior now. Here she was, mixed up in some sort of smuggling caper, and the car she'd been driving the day before had been stolen along with all her worldly goods.

None of that seemed as important as what she'd shared with Nick in the past twelve hours. Her pink Eastern New Mexico University T-shirt might as well read: I Made Love to Nick Hooper All Night. Every movement brought a delicious twinge somewhere on her body that reminded her that Nick had tested all her systems and found them in excellent working order.

After the first kiss at the restaurant she'd guessed that Nick's abilities as a lover would be considerable. Her previous experience hadn't provided her with much of a yardstick, but she had a hunch she'd underestimated by a mile. He seemed pretty happy with her, too, but she didn't know what that meant with a man like Nick Hooper. Just because he didn't consider her right for Lance didn't necessarily mean he had any permanent romantic plans himself.

They'd shared a heck of an instant attraction; neither of them could deny that. But how far beyond that had Nick's thoughts traveled? She wasn't prepared to ask him yet and risk getting an answer she didn't want. For now, it would have to be enough to know that she'd been lucky to spend one long, lusty night with Nick.

Some women could go a lifetime without having a night like that.

She pushed open the glass door to the office and shoved her sunglasses to the top of her head.

"Checking out?" the desk clerk asked, his glance flicking over her and lingering a moment on the bare legs below the shorts.

"Yes." Laura stepped closer to the counter to block his view and produced her credit card.

"Everything was all right?" He punched numbers into a computer, and the printer rolled out a copy of the bill.

"Everything was fine." She covered her smile with her hand. The desk clerk's sneaky appraisal of her body told her he didn't need to know how fine.

"That's good. Mr. Hooper mentioned this was a special night for you two, a celebration of sorts."

Laura opened her eyes wide. "He said what?"

"Well . . ." The man smirked and handed her the bill. "He just specified that we mustn't disturb you, and he sort of hinted that the two of you wanted to be left very much alone."

Suspicion grew in Laura's mind. "Are you saying that he didn't ask for two rooms?"

"Two rooms?" The man blinked. "Why would he do that?"

Laura picked up the bill and read the description— *deluxe king.* "Yes, why indeed," she said; suspicion changed to anger. "So I assume you had other rooms available?"

"Not many. We had a regular double, one with two twins and this one. Mr. Hooper chose this one. I do hope you both liked it?"

"I think at least one of us liked it a lot," she said, signing the credit-card slip and ripping off her portion with unnecessary force. That manipulating rat. He'd told her they had no choice but to share a room. He'd forced her into close proximity with him. He'd *planned* everything. Her warm mood evaporated like dew on a morning rose.

"Well, uh, have a nice day." The desk clerk looked confused. Laura bade him a terse goodbye and headed out the door toward the white truck in the driveway.

The truck's motor was running—and so was hers. She opened the passenger door and climbed into the cab. "You lied to me."

"About what?" He'd put on aviator shades and wore a muscle shirt that he'd said he kept in the truck as an emergency change of clothes. The tight-fitting shirt showed off his tattoo, and with the sunglasses, for the first time he looked as if he might have been a member of a street gang, as if a coiled viper belonged on his arm, after all.

"You said they only had one room left!" She waved the receipt at him. "You conned me, Nick."

"Oh, that. Listen, I can explain. You see—"

"I think I do see. Did you have it all planned, to seduce me and get my cooperation on this thing with Lance?" She was breathing hard.

"Hold it right there, lady." He switched off the ignition and leaned one arm with deliberate care upon the steering wheel before he turned to face her.

She was tempted to slap him, but he intimidated her a little too much. Her fingers closed over the receipt instead, crumpling it.

"In the first place," he began, speaking with maddening calm, "I didn't seduce you. The seduction was mutual. Or are you going to play the morning-after game and claim I'm the lousy guy who led you astray?"

Laura swallowed. This was a different Nick, an all-business Nick behind those darn sunglasses. And he was right about the lovemaking. "Okay. We participated equally, but none of that would have happened if we'd been in separate rooms. You set that up on purpose, which makes me feel manipulated." Now she felt like crying. She wouldn't cry. She wouldn't.

He didn't flinch at her accusation. He sat there silent, his dark glasses a barrier between them, his mouth grim. Then he sighed and took off the glasses. His gaze was troubled. "I did that because I didn't know if you were in on the smuggling, and I couldn't risk letting you out of my sight. Are you sorry about last night?"

She couldn't look him in the eye and say she was the least bit sorry. Yet the deception marred what had been a perfect memory, and she was furious with him for destroying her dream. "I guess I don't like the idea that you wanted to play on my attraction to you to find out the truth."

"I don't blame you." His tone grew gentler. "But if it makes you feel any better, Laura, it didn't work the way

I'd planned. I wanted to loosen your tongue with wine, and maybe some kisses, while I stayed in control and got my answers. Instead, once you were in my arms, I was a goner. I didn't care about the smuggling anymore."

Laura's anger began to fade. "Some spy you are, Nick Hooper."

"No kidding."

"I wouldn't go into espionage work if I were you, especially if it involves prying secrets from women."

"Woman," he corrected. "One woman. You. Believe it or not, this isn't the way I usually spend my evenings, or my mornings. There's something about you, Laura. I'm not even sure what it is. Maybe the way you smell, the way that little dimple flashes at the corner of your mouth, the way your eyes get all dark brown and dreamy. See, they're starting to get like that now. Laura, I'm sorry. I meant everything I said last night, everything I did."

She couldn't resist him, not when she looked into his eyes and remembered how it had felt to kiss him.

"Laura..." He leaned toward her. She leaned toward him.

Behind them someone honked. They both looked back and saw a motor home that would never pass through the space between the truck and the opposite curb. They smiled regretfully at each other and Nick started the engine. He replaced his sunglasses, and so did she before they pulled out of the driveway. Laura took his hand and they rode in silence to the wrecking yard.

A squad car sat beside the trailer office. Two uniformed officers and an attendant from the yard were busy pacing off the gaping hole in the cyclone fence and studying tire tracks. Laura picked out the spot where the Cadillac had been parked the night before. She'd hoped the dogs would have been taken away and was relieved not to see their bodies anywhere. She shivered in the sun and glanced at Nick. In his shades, jaw clenched and mouth set in a thin line, he looked tough enough to take on the world. She might even still be a little afraid of him herself, but knew how the eyes behind the shades could grow soft and gentle at a word or touch from her.

The attendant, a balding man in a white T-shirt, spotted them beside the truck and hurried over. "I was beginning to worry about you two, after you said you'd be right here."

Nick cleared his throat. "We, ah, needed to have some . . . breakfast."

Laura focused on the deep tracks and bare ground beneath her feet and worked very hard not to blush. She didn't succeed, and when she looked up, found the attendant staring at her.

He glanced away immediately. "You said the car didn't belong to you, miss." He gestured toward the now-empty parking space. "Do you have the name and number of the owner? We have insurance, of course. We can make this right, but we need to call the owners and let them know the circumstances."

Laura checked Nick's response with a quick look. When he nodded, she opened her purse and took out a slip of paper. "His name is Harold Atkins, and this is the number I've used to contact him. His address in San Francisco is on there, too."

"Fine." The man accepted the slip of paper and studied it. "I'll call right away. Either of you care for a cup of coffee?"

"No, thanks," Laura said.

Nick shook his head. "Thanks, anyway."

As the attendant left, one of the officers approached Laura. "I understand you were driving the car up to San Francisco for the owner. Is that right?"

Laura nodded.

"And you had it towed here when it wouldn't start at a restaurant in Big Sur?"

"Yes. My friend Nick Hooper drove down and tried to help, but he couldn't get it started, either."

The officer looked at both of them before returning his attention to the mangled fence. "Any idea why someone would go to so much trouble to steal the car? Any of your belongings worth that kind of effort?" He glanced back at Laura.

"No," Laura said, deciding this might be a good topic to divert the questioning. "I'll be glad to list what was in there, if you need to know."

"Go ahead." The officer took a pad of paper from his hip pocket and clicked a ballpoint pen with his thumb.

"Well, clothes, of course. Three business suits, several blouses, skirts, pairs of slacks. Sweaters, shoes, a winter coat. Then sports clothes—shorts, jeans, halter tops, sweatshirts, T-shirts, stuff like that."

The man wrote them down. "Normal, not designer?"

Laura chuckled. "Definitely not designer. Then a portable stereo unit, worth less than two hundred dollars, some pots and pans, a few dishes, glasses and silverware."

"Valuable silverware?"

"No. Odds and ends. And that's about it."

The officer scratched his ear with the clip on the ballpoint. "The car itself was expensive, a target, you could say, but cars like that are parked on the streets of Monterey all the time. Why mow down a fence and kill two dogs to get this particular one?"

"I don't know." Laura knew Nick was listening to her answers. She hoped she sounded convincing.

The officer tapped his notebook. "That's it?"

Laura nodded.

"Sure you haven't forgotten something?"

The attendant came running out, waving the slip of paper. "That number you gave me's been disconnected. Then I called Information and asked for the number of a Harold Atkins at the address you have here, and they said there was nobody at that address with that name."

The officer glanced sharply at Laura. "When did you say you called him last?"

Laura moved closer to Nick. So Atkins wasn't the man's name at all. After everything that had happened, she shouldn't be surprised. Yet confirmation that he was not who he'd pretended to be sent chills running through her.

Nick put an arm around her waist. "She called him last night and told him the car would be towed to Monterey. He wasn't very pleasant about the delay."

"Hmm." The officer glanced over his shoulder at his partner. "You about finished, Bill?" When his partner nodded, the officer stuck the notepad into his hip pocket and clipped the pen to his shirt pocket. "I'd like you two to follow me down to the station, if you don't mind. We'll take both your statements, and then you can continue on to San Francisco, but we'll need an address and phone number where we can reach you both."

"Sure," Nick said, giving Laura's waist a reassuring squeeze. "No problem. We'll follow you."

They climbed back into the truck and closed the doors. Laura glanced at the air vent near Nick's left foot. "I'm nervous," she admitted.

Nick put the truck into gear and followed the squad car out of the yard. "You can tell them anything you want," he said, taking her hand. "Remember that."

"And get you in trouble."

"That's my problem, not yours. Tell them I held you hostage. I'd never blame you, Laura. As I said before, this isn't your fight."

She looked at him, her gaze lingering on his profile. *Oh, yes, it is. I'm falling in love, which makes your fight mine.* "I won't tell them anything we haven't agreed on," she said. "Not even that Lance set me up with Atkins. If I mention that, they'll try to find Lance, to question him."

"Yes, they will."

"Then I'll just say Atkins came to the bank where I worked and asked if I was interested in driving his car to San Francisco, which is true, as far as it goes."

"Look, Laura. If this gets sticky, if it seems they've figured out there was something illegal in that car, don't admit you knew about it. If I hadn't told you, you wouldn't know, so just pretend I didn't tell you, okay?"

"No."

"No? What do you want to do, woman, get yourself thrown in jail?"

"If that's what will happen to you, yes."

He shook his head. "Lance told me you were a smart woman. I have my doubts."

"Shut up, Nick," she said softly. "Nobody's going to figure out anything." She looked at the air vent again. "I do wish we knew what it was, though."

"I don't think it's pot. I can't imagine people going crazy like this for a little bundle of marijuana. The stuff ain't that great."

"You've smoked it?"

He glanced at her. "Still don't get the picture about me, do you?"

"I'm beginning to. What else have you done, or should I even ask?"

"You want to know what I've actually done, or what's on my record? The two aren't the same. Thank God they didn't catch me on half the stuff, or P. Delwood Chambers would have more of a case against me than he already does."

She clutched his arm. "Nick, what if the police here probe into your background?"

He shrugged. "Fourteen-year-old offenses won't get them too excited. I've led an exemplary life since then, not even a traffic ticket."

"I've never even had a traffic ticket in my whole life."

"Sure you should be hooked up with a rough character like me? Might ruin your reputation."

Laura leaned back. "Now that I think about it, I probably had ruining my reputation in mind when I left Clovis. I'm tired of always being so safe and sound, Nick, so perfect and law-abiding. I want adventure."

Nick stopped behind the squad car at a red light. He turned to study Laura and sighed; the light turned green and they continued through the intersection. "I was afraid of that."

She was about to ask him what he meant when they arrived at the station.

BENNY STAYED three cars behind the white Hooper Carpentry truck after it left the wrecking yard, but didn't think he'd be recognized, anyway. He'd found a blond curly wig in a novelty shop the night before, after the incident when the guy called Nick had almost caught him. The wig and a shawl wrapped around his shoulders made Benny look like a bleached-blond grandmother with a day-old beard. He hadn't shaved and he was tired.

Sleeping in the car hadn't been the worst of it. He'd had to wake up every two hours and check on them, like checking on a baby. They'd had quite a night together, judging from the noises he'd heard through the door. Then this morning he'd waited until his stomach ached from hunger, while they fooled around some more before driving to the wrecking yard. On the way they'd passed two donut shops and a bakery. It had taken all his willpower to drive by, too.

At the wrecking yard he'd parked across the street and slithered down in the seat the minute he saw the squad car. When he'd worked up enough courage to peer over the doorframe, he'd noticed the big hole in the fence. The Cadillac was gone, and all Benny knew was that he hadn't taken it. He'd wanted to call the boss right then, but hadn't dared get out of the car.

Hungry and tired, his scalp itching from the blond wig, he waited until the squad car and the white truck left. He followed them to the police station, and when he was sure they were going inside, sped around the corner to a pay phone. He jerked his green sedan to a stop and leapt out, still wearing the wig and shawl.

When he got the recorded message telling him the phone had been disconnected, he nearly passed out. Here he was, all alone, with the car gone, probably the mask gone, and Lord knows who on his trail. He took the quarter out of the return slot. The only thing left to do was call his wife.

"Benny, where you been?" Erma complained in her high, squeaky voice. Benny loved her voice. It reminded him of Betty Boop.

"Business, honey."

"My brother's been here since nine o'clock, asking for you."

Benny sagged against the side of the booth in relief. His boss hadn't left him in the lurch, after all.

"Here he is," Erma said.

"Benny, you idiot!"

Benny jumped. "Yes, boss?"

"Why didn't you call earlier? You knew the phone would be disconnected by nine o'clock, and I'd be out of that house. Why didn't you call before then?"

"I forgot about that, boss. Besides, the girl and this guy, Lance's brother, were shacked up in the room until ten."

"I don't give a damn about that. Have you seen that double-crossing Lance Hooper?"

"Lance? No, boss. Is he the one who stole the Caddy?"

"*What?*"

Benny held the phone away from his ear as loud obscenities poured from the receiver. When the cursing stopped and he heard his name called several times, he chanced holding the receiver a little closer.

"Tell me about it, Benny," the tired voice said.

Benny told him.

"Well, it sure as hell wasn't Lance Hooper who stole that car. He's the wimpiest little prep-school type I've ever seen. Must have been Robles."

"R-Robles, boss?" Benny felt faint again. "Maybe I'll just drive on home now. Not much to do here, y'know."

"Yeah, you might as well. My sister's giving me fits about you being out of town, anyway. On the way up, keep an eye out for that little red sporty job Lance Hooper drives, will you? I sent him down there last night to get the mask. I think the son of a bitch double-crossed us, Benny. I think he's got it and plans to sell it himself, cut us out of the action."

"You mean it's not in the car Robles stole?"

"Probably not."

"When Robles finds out, he's gonna be mad, boss. He'll be looking for anybody connected to that car, like the girl and Lance's brother."

"Serves them right, Benny. Now get your ass home. Maybe we can find Lance Hooper before he makes the deal."

As LAURA LEFT the police station with Nick, she noticed a green car go by with a peculiar-looking woman driving it. The woman had frizzy blond hair and a shawl draped over her shoulders. Nick took Laura's arm and hurried her toward the truck. "What's the rush?" she asked, wanting to point the woman out to him. Although Nick had dawdled in the hotel room, toward the end of the questioning at the police station he'd kept glancing at his watch.

Nick unlocked her side of the truck. "I expected to be on the road by noon, and it's ten after. But I guess we'll be okay."

"What difference does it make?" She climbed into the sun-warmed cab.

"I just want to get this drive over with," he said, gazing at her. "That stuff in the air vent is making me nervous."

"At least the police questioning wasn't bad. They didn't dig into your past record or anything."

"No." He glanced back. "But they're not finished with us, or this case. They're suspicious, and they'll keep an eye on us until the whole thing's cleared up or goes away."

"You really think it's drugs, don't you?"

"Yeah." He slammed the truck door and rounded the cab to the driver's side. "They might suspect something like that, too," he said, fitting the key into the ignition. He peered into the rearview mirror and backed the truck into the traffic.

"What will we do with it, Nick, after we get back to your place?"

"I don't know. If it is drugs, and Lance is responsible for having them delivered . . . Well, we won't worry about that yet."

"About what?"

Nick hesitated. "I've known of people getting killed because they didn't deliver the goods entrusted to them."

"No!" Laura stared at him, horrified. "You mean we can't just flush them down the toilet?"

"Maybe not. I told you this could get rough. It's not too late, Laura. I can still get you a ticket out of this mess."

For one brief moment she was tempted, then imagined going home again, trying to regain her job at the bank, admitting defeat after her attempt at independence. "No," she said. "I'm staying."

"Every instinct I have tells me to convince you otherwise."

She glanced at him. "It would be a waste of breath."

"I should amend that." He gave her a long look. "Every instinct but one."

He returned his attention to the road, and a heightened awareness settled between them. He reached over and took her hand. She couldn't leave him. Not yet. Not until she knew if they had a chance together.

He stopped at a red light. "There's a hamburger place across the street. Maybe we should grab some food on the way out of town."

"I'm not very hungry."

"Neither am I, but we don't know what's ahead of us. Too bad we can't stay here and enjoy Monterey. It has some great restaurants where you can watch the otters while you eat, but this isn't the time." He turned into the parking lot.

She felt a tug at her heart. If life were arranged to suit her, they'd watch those cute little otters and check into another hotel for the night. There would be no mysterious package in the air vent, no Lance to deal with, no commitments. They'd have time to explore what was happening between them as man and woman, not as fellow conspirators. She wished Nick would at least say that they'd be back someday, but he didn't. Neither of them had made any statements like that, promises that reached into an uncertain future—as if they had to get past the immediate problems first. She hoped that would be soon.

They ate cheeseburgers and sipped chocolate milk shakes while Nick drove them past million-dollar homes that faced the ocean. The view was on Nick's side of the truck, so she had a perfect excuse to gaze in his direction. They'd left the windows rolled down and the breeze ruffled his brown hair.

He glanced over and caught her staring.

"Nice view," she said.

"Prime real estate." He returned his attention to the road.

You bet. Every masculine inch of territory on your body. She took a deep breath of the salty air and let her imagination go. She wished she and Nick were driving home to one of the luxurious houses nestled below the road, surrounded by wind-twisted cypress trees, so that only the cedar-shake roofline showed. As the homes flashed by she occasionally glimpsed a path leading to a private stretch of beach. She could almost feel the sand beneath her bare feet, its shifting surface giving way to the cool resilience of the wet sand at the water line.

No clouds marred the arch of sky, and the ocean glinted in the sunlight. The water fanned out like tie-dyed silk—shimmering pale sapphire over the sandbars, aquamarine marking the deeper troughs, and a gray-blue lining the horizon. Whitecaps dotted the surface like bits of torn tissue paper. Faced with such beauty, Laura couldn't hold on to her fantasy. It seemed impossibly out of reach.

Nick glanced at her again. "You look like a kid at the candy-store window."

"I feel like one. No matter how hard I try, I have a tough time imagining myself rich enough to afford to live in one of these houses."

"It takes a lot of work and a lot of luck. Unless, of course, you opt for a shortcut, like Lance."

Laura came back to earth with a thud. For a moment she'd forgotten all about Lance and the predicament they were in. "Nick, we're still not sure. Maybe . . ."

"Yeah, maybe he was kidnapped by aliens. Maybe he decided to enlist in the marines. Maybe he joined some religious—" Nick gripped the wheel and glanced into the rearview mirror. "Dammit," he swore softly.

"What?" Laura almost dropped her cheeseburger. "What's the matter?"

Nick glanced in the rearview mirror. "I was afraid of this. Somebody's tailing us."

7

"YOU MEAN THE POLICE?" Laura started to turn around.

"No. And don't look back," Nick said. "I don't want him to know I'm aware of him. Just check your side mirror and tell me if you recognize the car or the driver."

Heart pounding, Laura leaned toward the mirror. A sinister black Firebird, the hood covered with rust, was behind them. Mud coated the bottom half of the car and covered the license plate. A windshield smeared with bugs partially obscured the driver, but Laura saw dark glasses and a baseball cap. He could have been almost anyone.

"That's one ugly means of transportation," she murmured.

"Anyone you know?"

"Not that I can tell. I can't see the driver very well, but there's nothing familiar about him."

"Could it be Atkins, or whatever the guy's name is?"

Laura looked again. "Not unless he shaved off his mustache. No, I don't think it's him. Atkins wears a cowboy hat all the time."

"So it's not the fat little guy, either?"

"Definitely not him. He had a double chin." Laura watched the car hold steady behind them. "How do you know he's following us? Maybe he just happens to be there."

"I've been varying my speed. He varies his. Twice I've passed cars where there was just enough room for me, and he's squeezed around, too. I don't think it's by chance."

Beads of moisture prickled on Laura's upper lip. "What should we do?"

"Nothing yet. This truck sure as hell can't outrun a car like that."

Laura couldn't take her attention from the reflection in the side mirror. The low-slung car lurked ominously, tracking them like a battle-scarred panther. "He's after the stuff in the air vent." She whispered the words, although there was no chance the man in the black car could overhear her.

"No doubt."

"But he'll have to pull us over to get it." Her stomach churned as she imagined the scene. Guns and blood. Bonnie and Clyde. "Don't let him pull us over, Nick."

"I won't. At least the truck's built for abuse. His fiberglass baby may be fast, but she'll crumple if he tries to get rough."

"Then we're pretty safe?"

"Not necessarily. We've been lucky to have plenty of traffic so far. He may be waiting for a lonely stretch so he can shoot at the tires."

"Oh, God!" Laura put her hand over her mouth.

"I should have sent you back to Clovis," Nick muttered. "I'm a damn fool for putting you in danger like this. I must have been thinking with my—"

"Nick, it's okay," she said, recovering. "I'm really not all that scared."

"Liar. You turned white as a sheet."

"Okay, I'm scared. But I'd still rather be here, no matter what happens, than driving some rental car back to Clovis. I'll see this thing through." She took a deep breath. "I will, Nick."

"Unfortunately, you don't have much choice." He clenched his jaw. "Hang on. I'm going to try and ditch him."

Laura clutched the armrest as Nick slammed the gas pedal to the floor. The truck lurched around the car in front of them, throwing her against the shoulder harness. In the other lane a van bore down on them, its horn blaring. Laura screamed. Nick made it into the right lane with inches to spare.

"Please don't kill us, Nick," Laura pleaded.

"That wasn't as dangerous as it looked. God, if this doesn't feel like the bad old days." He careened around a curve, making the tires squeal and his ladders crash against each other in the truck bed. "Dammit, he's forcing me to throw my equipment around. He just might irritate me yet."

Laura glanced at Nick and almost didn't recognize him as the same man who'd loved her so tenderly only hours before. His expression held the fierce determination of a warrior. This Nick didn't look gentle; he looked dangerous. Ahead of them a motor home lumbered along the road. Laura closed her eyes, while Nick gunned the motor and veered around. Once more a horn blasted them; once more they emerged on the other side, safely back in the right lane.

She opened her eyes and looked into the side mirror. "He's still there!"

"I know. What in the hell is so important in this air vent, anyway? I'm taking chances, but this guy's driving like a maniac!"

Laura made up her mind that she was probably going to die. Twice they'd almost had a head-on collision. Nick's pressure on the gas pedal hadn't let up, and his luck wouldn't hold out forever. As they sped along the road, the traffic gradually lightened and the Firebird edged closer.

"Keep an eye on him, Laura," Nick said.

The muddy grille loomed in the mirror. The driver rolled down his window and slowly eased the muzzle of a gun along the doorframe. Laura watched in horror. "He has a gun out," she said, her throat tight with fear. "Can you go any faster?"

"No. Dammit, where's my reinforcements?"

"Reinforcements?" Laura heard a pop and saw a puff of smoke. "Nick, he's firing!"

"Let's hope he's not a very good shot," Nick said through clenched teeth; he glanced into the rearview mirror. "Let's hope— Wait a minute. Wait a minute! Here they come!"

"Who? The police?" Laura turned and looked back and saw two—no, four—motorcycles closing the gap behind the Firebird.

"In this case, better than the police. He sees them, too, I'll bet. He's stopped firing."

Four cycles came on in formation, their gleaming chrome flashing in the sun. The men rode low, settled back like kings on their thrones. They wore silver-studded black leather, and bandannas held their long hair from their faces. Laura turned back to Nick. "The Vipers?" she whispered.

"Banjo and Deadline took their damn time. They're lucky I still know how to drive."

"Banjo and Deadline?"

"My two closest friends in the gang."

"So you knew about this?"

He nodded. "Insurance policy. Wasn't sure I'd need it."

Laura concentrated on the side mirror. Now the driver of the Firebird seemed anxious to pass Nick, but every time he tried, Nick moved in front of him, blocking his way. The cycles drew closer, the rumble of their engines growing louder. Laura noticed that the bike in front, closest to the shoulder of the road, carried two riders; the man on the back held a baseball bat across his knees.

Moving as a unit, the four cyclists surged around the Firebird and held steady, just long enough for the man with the bat to smash the Firebird's windshield. The car swerved to the edge of the road and ploughed into a speed-limit sign.

Laura whooped. "They got him!" They rounded a curve and the wrecked car disappeared from view.

"Looks like Deadline hasn't lost his technique." Nick shoved his arm out the window and raised his fist in salute. The lead rider returned the gesture.

"Deadline was the one with the bat?"

"Yep. Banjo drove the cycle, which isn't so easy, either. Your timing has to be perfect, and balancing that Harley while someone's swinging a baseball bat—both of you can end up as road kill, ground under the wheels of the car."

"You sound like you know what you're talking about."

"Don't ask me to try something like that now."

"But you've done it," she persisted. "Which were you, the driver or the one with the bat?"

"I didn't use a bat."

A picture of Nick's license plate flashed into Laura's head. So the plate was more than an advertisement for his business. He hadn't completely let go of his days with the gang. "How ironic that you became a carpenter," she said, trying to imagine him wielding a hammer from the back of a Harley.

He grimaced. "I always was good with tools."

"Their names, Banjo and Deadline, where did they come from?"

"It's not very complicated. Banjo plays a banjo, believe it or not." Nick paused. "Although I think he ripped if off of someone when he was about fourteen," he added with a wry smile. "Deadline was the one who kept everyone informed of news and rumors about other gangs, sort of like a reporter."

"I see." Laura registered a smile of nostalgia on Nick's face. He'd had some good times in the gang, as well as some bad ones. She weighed what she wanted to say and finally decided to chance it. "You know, Nick, I'm not making excuses for Lance's behavior, assuming he's in on the smuggling, but have you ever thought how he must idolize you?"

"Idolize me?" Nick snorted with derision. "I've spent fourteen years trying to live down the stupid mistakes I made. Some idol."

"Yes, but you were tough, powerful. You and your gang were a law unto yourselves, and you were good friends, with unshakable loyalty. Maybe Lance envies that."

Nick sighed. "Yeah, I guess it's possible. I've tried to tell him what a dumb jerk I was back then, but maybe he sees it differently, glamorizes it."

Laura took another look at the motorcycles behind them. The men riding them were muscular and intimidating. "Wouldn't be hard to glamorize," she said. "That rescue was pretty exciting, even admirable, under the circumstances."

"I've got to talk to that kid, square him away," Nick said. "I just hope it isn't too late."

"If you want to disenchant him, I wouldn't spend too much time on this incident." She nodded toward the squadron of cyclists. "Will they follow us all the way to San Francisco?"

"I don't know. Banjo and Deadline may. They've always been protective of me. I don't recognize the other three guys. New, probably. Banjo said something on the phone about hanging around for a few days until this problem is solved."

"Hanging around at your house?"

Nick shook his head. "Nope. I offered, but he's worried about my reputation. They'll just melt into the background, I guess, show up if they sense trouble. They— Well, I'll be damned! Look at that!"

Ahead of them four more motorcycles left a turnout and pulled in front of the truck.

"What are they doing?" Laura asked.

Nick laughed and relaxed against the seat. "Looks like Banjo didn't want to take any chances. We have ourselves an escort into the city, Laura."

THE PHALANX of eight motorbikes stayed with the truck until they reached the outskirts of San Francisco. Nick was silent as he drove, and Laura respected that. She imagined that the reappearance of his former gang members stirred up some powerful memories, and she didn't want to intrude on his thoughts.

The front four left first. She hated to see them go, but recognized the wisdom of their departure. With Nick's past record, he couldn't afford to be seen with members of his old gang, even in a city as large as San Francisco. If the wrong people noticed, his contractor's license would never go through. Besides, Laura was convinced Lance had already been influenced by Nick's previous behavior, more than either he or Nick might want to admit. The less Lance was exposed to this atmosphere, the better.

Soon Laura was absorbed in the glittering view of the city. She recognized the distinctive pyramid shape of the Transamerica Building and longed for a glimpse of the famous Golden Gate Bridge. From a map that Lance had marked for her she knew Nick wouldn't have to drive across that bridge to reach his house.

Carrying contraband wasn't part of Laura's original image of her introduction to San Francisco. Still, she was excited at arriving in the city.

"Pretty soon we'll find out what's in that blasted package," Nick said as he shifted into second gear to climb a steep hill.

"I don't know much about drugs," Laura told him. "Only that marijuana looks like oregano and cocaine is some sort of white powder."

"Well, I know more than I'd like to. I guess Lance forgot about the time one of the Vipers overdosed on a bad batch of speed. I intend to remind him as soon as I get the chance."

"Maybe he'll be at your place, waiting for us."

"That would be a break, but I wouldn't hold my breath." Nick swung the truck into a short driveway. The house had a shallow front yard and was Victorian in design, as were the others lining the hilly street. The builder had taken advantage of the slope by tucking a garage under the first floor of each house. They were all two and a half stories, with an attic under each peaked roof. Nick's neighbors had chosen various pastels for the outside of their homes, but Nick's house was forest green with white gingerbread trim.

"I like it," Laura said.

"Me, too."

She glanced down the street. "Where's the rest of your gang?"

NO RISK, NO OBLIGATION TO BUY...NOW OR EVER!

GUARANTEED

PLAY "ROLL A DOUBLE" AND GET AS MANY AS FIVE GIFTS!

HERE'S HOW TO PLAY:

1. Peel off label from front cover. Place it in space provided at right. With a coin, carefully scratch off the silver dice. This makes you eligible to receive two or more free books, and possibly another gift, depending on what is revealed beneath the scratch-off area.

2. You'll receive brand-new Harlequin Temptation® novels. When you return this card, we'll rush you the books and gift you qualify for ABSOLUTELY FREE!

3. Then, if we don't hear from you, every month, we'll send you 4 additional novels to read and enjoy. You can return them and owe nothing, but if you decide to keep them, you'll pay only $2.69 per book—a saving of 30¢ each off the cover price—plus only 49¢ delivery for the entire shipment.

4. When you subscribe to the Harlequin Reader Service®, you'll also get our newsletter, as well as additional free gifts from time to time.

5. You must be completely satisfied. You may cancel at any time simply by sending us a note or a shipping statement marked ''cancel'' or by returning any shipment to us at our expense.

The Austrian crystal sparkles like a diamond! And it's carefully set in a romantic "Key to Your Heart" pendant on a generous 18″ chain. The entire necklace is yours free as added thanks for giving our Reader Service a try!

HARLEQUIN "NO RISK" GUARANTEE

- You're not required to buy a single book—ever!
- You must be completely satisfied or you may cancel at any time simply by sending us a note or shipping statement marked "cancel" or by returning any shipment to us at our cost. Either way, you will receive no more books; you'll have no obligation to buy.
- The free books and gift you claimed on this "Roll A Double" offer remain yours to keep no matter what you decide.

If offer card is missing, please write to: Harlequin Reader Service, P.O. Box 609, Fort Erie, Ontario L2A 5X3

DETACH AND MAIL CARD TODAY!

"Banjo and Deadline are at the top of the next hill, keeping an eye on us. The others dropped away several blocks ago." Nick put the truck into neutral and set the hand brake. "No automatic door on this garage. Lock the cab after me and stay with the truck. I'll open up and check around before we drive in."

"Okay." She locked the door behind him and looked to the top of the next hill. Sure enough, a cycle was parked there with two men sitting on it, waiting. The Vipers were a loyal bunch, she'd give them that.

Nick reappeared and she snapped up the lock on the driver's side of the truck.

"All clear," he said, climbing in. "But it doesn't look like Lance has been around, either."

"That's not so good."

"No. If we don't find him in twenty-four hours, we'll call the police."

The inside of the garage had the musty smell of old wood mixed with the tang of fresh two-by-fours stacked along one wall. A sailboard was stored in the rafters. "You're renting this house?" Laura got out of the cab and retrieved her overnight bag and purse from the floor.

"Lease-purchase." Nick left his door open and flicked on an overhead shop light. "I worked out a deal with the owner. The place needed some renovation, so I'm putting in sweat equity and keeping track of my materials and labor. When I've made enough improvements to be equivalent to a down payment, my rent checks will become mortgage payments."

"Creative."

"Thanks." He closed the garage door and turned the handle, locking it. "Now let's find out what's in that air vent." Nick took a screwdriver off a Peg-Board on the garage wall.

Carrying her bag and purse, Laura walked around the tailgate and stood near him as he crouched beside the driver's seat. "And to think you had me believing that story about the clutch pedal."

"Yeah." He glanced up. "I didn't know if you'd seen me transfer the package, so I must have jumped a mile when you spoke to me."

Laura set down her things and leaned against the side of the truck. "Actually you were pretty cool. I guess you've had practice in handling tough situations."

"Unfortunately." He turned back to the air vent. "Although I'm not very proud of it."

She watched him take the screws out of the vent cover. Pleasure zinged through her at the sight of his capable hands at work, hands that had given her so much joy. But when he pulled the package out and laid it upon the seat of the truck, the back of Laura's neck prickled. Until she saw the package lying there, the smuggling hadn't seemed quite real to her. The heavy-duty padded envelope closed with industrial staples looked like many she'd received from mail-order houses. Except this wasn't a delivery from UPS. A wave of dread constricted her throat.

"Hand me that utility knife hanging on the Peg-Board," Nick asked, getting to his feet.

She found it easily. He was a neat craftsman. He carefully sliced open one side of the package, then reached in and pulled out something wrapped in tissue paper. "I don't get it," he said, unwinding the tissue paper. "This doesn't feel like— Lord Almighty! What the hell *is* that?"

Laura stared at the plastic-wrapped object he held in his hand. The abalone shell glittered under the fluorescent shop light. The face was perfectly proportioned, the clay faded to the color of rich cream. The newspaper photograph hadn't done justice to the real thing. "It's the mask," she said in awe. "The Anasazi mask."

"You *know* what this is? Laura, I thought you had nothing to do with—"

"I don't. I read about it in the paper yesterday." She remembered her reaction to the picture. Looking at the mask now, she felt a sense of kinship.

"In the paper?" Nick's eyes narrowed.

"Yes. If you still have an afternoon edition from yesterday, I can prove it to you. While I was waiting for you to show up I bought a newspaper. A picture of this mask was on the front page. Somebody stole it from a dig in New Mexico. It's worth a lot of money."

"Then Atkins stole it, or somebody who works for him."

"I guess so. This explains a lot. The dig wasn't far from Clovis. If the car hadn't broken down, I'd have delivered it, and this mask, yesterday. Atkins probably has a contact here in San Francisco who will pay him for it."

"How much?"

"The paper said it's worth at least two million dollars."

"The hell you say!" Nick quickly held on to the mask with both hands.

"Don't drop it."

"I don't even want to hold it. Here, you take it."

"All right." She put out her hands, and Nick laid the mask gently upon them. The clay felt cool and dry. She turned the face around so that she was gazing into the sightless eyes. "There's something wonderful about this," she said. "Something almost . . . magical."

"I should hope to Hannah there is, if someone's putting that kind of value on it. Personally I'd say it belongs in a garage sale."

"You don't think it's beautiful?"

"No. You're beautiful. That's dried mud. No comparison. Here, let's wrap it up again and put it back in the truck. I can't think of a safer place for the time being." She returned the mask and he began wrapping the tissue paper around it. "Thank God it's not what I thought it would be! I was trying to figure out how I'd live with myself if I helped Lance deliver his shipment of cocaine, knowing what that junk does to people. Stolen merchandise is bad enough, but drugs . . ." He shuddered.

"I know." She hadn't realized how tense she'd been about the possibility of drugs until now.

"When we find Lance," Nick continued, "we can also find out what the heck he was supposed to do with this. If he'll testify against Atkins and tell who the potential buyer is, maybe he'll get off with a lighter sentence." He slid the package into the air vent and replaced the louvered cover. "Come on." He picked up her overnight bag. "Let's go inside."

With a sense of anticipation Laura followed Nick up two concrete steps and through a door. They would be alone in this house. Of course, they had to concentrate on finding Lance, but now she would see where Nick lived, how he lived. They'd have to sleep sometime, and then . . . in the privacy of Nick's bedroom . . . Her heart beat faster.

"We don't cook around here," Nick said as they walked through an unfinished kitchen with cabinet doors taken off their hinges and plastic sheeting thrown over the appliances. "The refrigerator works, and the coffeemaker, but that's about it."

He paused in a sparsely furnished living room with bay windows that overlooked the street. Mail had been shoved through a slot in the door. "That's how I know Lance hasn't been here. He wouldn't have left the mail like that."

Laura glanced around at the faded rose wallpaper and the scuffed floor covered by a worn rug. The window casings had been sanded and painted a pale green. The house was old, but she could imagine how it would look when Nick finished the restoration. "It's a nice house."

"It will be." He motioned down a short hallway. "Lance's bedroom is on this floor and mine's upstairs." He paused and gazed at her. "I've been doing some thinking, Laura. Maybe you should stay in Lance's room."

The words hit her like a slap. Her dreams crumbled. "Why?" she cried, too hurt to think of salvaging her pride.

"Because you were right," he said gently. "Lance has used me as a role model, and that makes me responsible for helping him through this. He'll have to trust me, and how can I expect him to do that if I have one hand out to him and the other around his girlfriend?"

8

"His girlfriend?" Laura couldn't believe Nick had said it. "But I'm not his girlfriend!"

"You were," he said quietly. "He needs my help. Is he going to want it if he thinks I took you away from him?"

Laura stared at him, too stunned to speak. She had done this, planted this thought in Nick's head by suggesting he'd been a big influence on Lance's behavior. Now he didn't want anything standing in the way when he tried to help Lance out of this mess. And she was standing in the way.

"Lance's bedroom is down the hall." He walked toward a door and pushed it open.

Laura followed, still dazed by the sudden turn of events. Nick paused in the doorway, muttered an oath and strode forward to pick a metal carpenter's level off the floor. Rumpled black sheets covered an unmade double bed, and clothes were scattered everywhere— draped over an easy chair, hanging out of open dresser drawers, in heaps on the floor. "Nick, the room's been ransacked!" Laura cried. "Maybe somebody—"

He turned. "No, it's always like this. On top of that he borrows my tools and never puts them away. Didn't you ever see his apartment in Clovis?" Nick's expression was closed and hard. "I'm sure it was the same."

"I was never in his apartment," she said. "He never invited me there. Now I guess I know why." She hesitated, then moved resolutely into the room.

"Wait." He blocked her way with the level. "You're not sleeping in this pigsty. You can have my room and I'll sleep here."

"No." If Nick was going to push her away, she didn't want to be trapped with the sensuous images that would assault her in his bedroom.

His eyes darkened. "Don't argue with me. We both know you don't belong in a place like this."

"Then where do I belong, Nick?"

She knew that battle raged within him as his jaw clenched. One answer in particular would hurl them into each other's arms. "Come upstairs" was all he said.

She went, not because she was giving in, but because Nick might be. He left the level at the bottom of the stairs and started up. She followed, running her hand along the polished mahogany banister. She imagined him rubbing the wood smooth, and her body ached from wanting him. In a very short time his touch had become essential to her.

At the top of the stairs she paused. Nick's bedroom was straight ahead, and to her left was a large open space where he must have knocked out some walls to create his office. French doors opened onto a balcony, and beyond, over the rooftops was the view of the city. She walked toward the open bedroom door where Nick waited, like an eagle in his aerie, she thought.

He stood aside and allowed her to enter. A pair of double-hung windows presented the same view as the balcony. A massive walnut four-poster was positioned to take advantage of the view, which promised to be even more spectacular at night. The giant bed left only enough space in the room for a matching dresser. A braided rug lay at the side of the bed on the refinished oak floor. A green-and-white striped comforter was tucked around the mattress, and several pillows with white cases were stacked against the headboard.

Laura walked over and ran her hand along the curved footboard of the bed, then turned back and found Nick leaning against the doorframe and watching her. His arms were folded. She might have been fooled into thinking he was relaxed until she gazed into his eyes. Their gray depths were turbulent with unspoken emotion.

"The bathroom's through there," he said, indicating an open door along the wall to her right.

She didn't follow the motion of his hand, but held him captive with her eyes. "I love your house." She could say that much. He obviously wouldn't want to hear that she was falling in love with the man who was restoring it.

His hands curled into fists. She remembered how much he'd wanted her only hours before. Denying himself now appeared to require almost superhuman control. Her gaze moved slowly over him; she willed him to give up this crazy self-sacrifice. She saw his chest rise and fall as his breathing quickened. Lower still, his arousal strained the fabric of his jeans.

"Dammit, Laura," he groaned and started toward her.

A telephone rang in the next room, halting him in midstride.

Laura gripped the bedpost. "It could be Lance." Heaven help her, she wanted him to let it ring.

"Yes." He turned and left.

Lance. He'd brought them together. Now it seemed he would keep them apart. She followed Nick out the door.

The room contained an old but comfortable-looking couch, a large, battered desk and wooden swivel chair, two unmatched end tables with lamps, and a drafting table and stool.

The phone was on Nick's desk. "Yes, she's right here," he said, and covered the mouthpiece with his hand. "It's your mother. Don't worry. I told her you had some unexpected delays and didn't have much chance to use the phone."

Laura had completely forgotten about her parents. Of course, they'd be worried. Contrite, she braced herself for the barrage of questions she would face. "Mom? I'm really sorry I didn't call. I know you've been worried."

"Worried isn't the word for it, Laura." Her mother's tone was accusatory. "Your father and I didn't sleep a wink all night. Well, I take that back. Your father slept. You know how he snores. I kept trying to call you at Lance's but I kept getting that machine. You know I hate those machines. So I'd just hang up."

"Next time, Mom, please leave a message. Then I'll be sure and get back to you."

"I don't think I can get used to those machines," her mother said. "Anyway, you're there now. Lance's brother said you had some car trouble and he had to go down to Monterey to help you out. Why didn't Lance drive down to help?"

"Well, Lance isn't here. He . . . had this seminar, for the bank."

"Oh, really? Such an up-and-comer, that Lance. When will he be back?"

"Umm, soon." Laura had forgotten how much her mother liked Lance. Her parents' approval had gone a long way toward helping them accept her decision to move.

"I'll bet when that boy comes back he'll have a ring in his pocket, Laura. You'd better call us right away when you two set the date. You'll have the ceremony here in Clovis, of course. I'll help you make the arrangements, but we'll need plenty of time, dear."

"You're jumping the gun a little," Laura said. Nick had walked out onto the balcony and was leaning on the railing. Laura admired the strong breadth of his shoulders and the narrow span of his hips. "Lance never actually proposed, you know. Marriage could be a ways off for both of us."

"Nonsense. Lance recognizes what an asset you'd be to him in his career. He's a smart boy."

Her mother never thought in terms of what would be an asset to *Laura's* career, she reflected. Lance hadn't been much concerned, either, come to think of it. But Nick was. "I'd better go, Mom," she said. "I still haven't unpacked."

"Goodness! You'd better do that. Clothes shouldn't stay crammed together in a damp climate like that. You'll have mildew in no time. Be sure you clean everything out of the back of that car, too. I don't imagine Mr. Atkins would appreciate finding odds and ends of yours in his nice new Cadillac."

Laura almost laughed out loud. What had happened to her clothes was probably way beyond mildew, and Mr. Atkins, or whoever he was, probably would have abandoned the Cadillac once the smuggling had been completed. But it was far better her mother believed that all was well.

"Right, Mom," she said. "See you later."

"Give my love to Lance," her mother said, then hung up.

Laura replaced the receiver. The phone rang again and she picked it up, thinking her mother must have forgotten something. Instead a woman with a low, seductive voice asked for Nick.

Bristling, and feeling ridiculous for doing so, Laura adopted her best receptionist's tone. "And who may I say is calling?"

"Joanne," the caller said. "Just tell him it's Joanne. He'll know."

Massaging a dull ache at her temples, Laura went to the door to call Nick in from the balcony.

LANCE SLAMMED the phone into its cradle and flung himself onto the brocade bedspread. The line was busy, dammit. He poured himself another glass of the French wine he'd ordered from room service. The wine was gradually easing the pain of his dog bite. Maybe he'd order another bottle.

But he needed to get through to Nick before that. At first all he could get was the blasted machine, and now either Nick or Laura must be gabbing on the telephone. At least they were home, finally. Now if they'd just stay off the damned line, he could get through. He didn't dare leave a message. Atkins hadn't had time to tap the phone, but he might break into the house somehow, in spite of Nick's fancy alarm system, and play any messages on the answering machine.

Lance tried Nick's number again. Still busy. He should have talked his stupid brother into signing up for call waiting, but Nick, being behind the times, hadn't wanted it. He'd remind Nick of that once they straightened this mess out. Lance had no doubt his brother would help him straighten it out. Nick had always taken care of him before, and besides, Nick knew about things like this.

He would probably be proud of Lance's strategy so far. Not everyone would have considered the possibility of hiding out at the Saint Francis. Of course, his Visa Gold Card had helped. After pumping several two-hundred-dollar cash advances from the automatic teller, he'd bought clothes and a suitcase. He'd parked the MR-2 in a public garage down by the Wharf and taken a cab to the hotel. Then he'd paid cash for his room; that had allowed him to register under any name he chose. He'd chosen Richard J. Quick.

Room service enabled him to eat without leaving his room. He was safe for now, but he had to talk to Nick.

Together they might be able to get the mask back from whoever had taken it. If Benny had it, he and Nick could outwit Benny any day in the week.

He needed to keep calling Nick, but he was tired, so very tired. He hadn't slept in about thirty-three hours. Now that the wine had taken away some of the pain in his leg and the room was securely locked, maybe he should get some sleep. He tried the number once more—still busy. Uttering a groan, he stretched out on the bed.

LAURA REFUSED to feel guilty for eavesdropping. She sat on the couch and picked up an *Architectural Digest* magazine lying on an end table. She flipped through the magazine without seeing it.

"I certainly believe that you called Mr. Chambers. I would even believe that he's offering to make things tough for my carpentry business. I can't help that, but I told you that I have a family emergency. I may not make it tomorrow. I'll have to let you know when I can complete the work." He paused. "Excuse me, but it's none of your business who answered the phone."

Laura realized Joanne had asked about her.

"I think that about ends our conversation, Joanne," Nick said. "Goodbye." He replaced the receiver and punched on the answering machine. The phone rang again immediately. Nick waited for the machine to answer with his Hooper Carpentry message.

After the beep, Joanne's husky voice filled the room. "I will not have my work delayed because you've decided to shack up with some two-bit floozy for a few days. And don't try and tell me that's not what you're doing. Delwood told me all about you—the car theft, and then stealing his son's fiancée. He says you're hell on wheels, and I'm not safe with you in the house, but you're a damned good carpenter, so I'm willing to risk it. In addition to that, I can use my influence with Delwood to get you that precious contractor's license. You're making a mistake, Hooper. Get your butt over here. Pronto." There was a click, and the telephone beeped again. A red light flashed, indicating the message. The room was silent.

"His son's fiancée?" Laura asked. "You failed to mention that part."

"I was young, Laura. Out to prove things." Nick walked to the French doors. Shoving his hands into his back pockets, he gazed out at the city. "Look, I know what you must be thinking, that last night was the same—taking something away from my little brother, to prove I'm a better man." He turned back to her. "That wasn't what last night was all about."

"I believe you."

The tense line of his shoulders relaxed a little. "Thanks. You don't know how much that means. I'm not the same person I was fourteen years ago."

"Oh, I wouldn't say that."

His expression became wary. "What do you mean?"

"You still have a streak of stubbornness in you, Nick, and you're still something of a rebel. You could have explained a little more of your situation to Joanne. She might have been more sympathetic if you'd said your brother was in some trouble and you needed to help him. You could have told her that much without endangering secrets."

"Joanne doesn't need to know anything."

"Doesn't she?" Laura studied him. Considering what a private man he was, she was amazed that he'd opened up as much as he had to her. "Sounds like if you played your cards right, you could have everything you want on a silver platter."

"If getting my contractor's license depends on taking Joanne to bed, I guess I'll be pounding nails and sawing boards for a long time to come."

"Maybe it wouldn't be like that."

He grimaced. "Judging from past experience, it would be exactly like that."

"Which is another thing that hasn't changed about you," Laura said. "Women apparently still find you irresistible, and it's still getting you in trouble."

His gaze lingered on her face. Then he shook his head and sighed. "We need to get out of here, for a number of reasons. The first one we won't discuss. The second is that the bank closes in fifteen minutes and I want to talk to a couple of people down there. Third, I need to rope Banjo and Deadline into this search. And last, I wondered if you wanted to stop by a department store for a few extra clothes. No telling if and when we'll get yours back."

Laura got up from the couch and glanced at her shorts and T-shirt. "That would be nice, if you're sure we have time."

"We'll make time."

"I don't browse. I'm a fast shopper."

"Somehow I knew that. Let's go." When she hesitated, he gazed deep into her eyes. "Please."

She turned and started down the staircase.

IT WAS SWEET TORTURE for Nick to watch her walk down the stairs, her white shorts cupping her firm behind. Her creamy thighs below the hem of the shorts made him ache with longing. Even the backs of her knees drove him crazy. His fingers trembled with the need to caress her, and his mouth moistened at the thought of kissing her. What he would give for one kiss. But one kiss wasn't possible with Laura Rhodes. Even on the restaurant deck, with people watching, he'd had a hell of a time restraining himself after the first sizzling encounter.

What a mess he was in—aching for a woman he ought not to want, and all because of his brother. How ironic that without Lance, Nick would never have experienced the intense passion he felt for Laura. Now, because of Lance, he couldn't make love to her—at least not until this was settled and Lance was on a different track.

Nick took his checkbook from a desk drawer and started after Laura. He followed her down the stairs and forced his mind away from her, concentrating on his little brother instead. The poor guy had probably crept into hiding when he'd discovered everything had gone wrong. Nick pictured him cowering in some flophouse, surrounded by rats and cockroaches. Lance was used to clutter, but not the kind of filth he'd find on the wrong side of town; he wouldn't know how to handle deprivation and fear. He'd never had to. Nick had to find him.

Laura was already in the truck when Nick swung open the garage door. He backed the truck out, secured the garage, and headed down the street to the opposite hill, where Banjo and Deadline waited near a stop sign. Pulling up at the sign, Nick glanced into his rearview mirror. When he saw no one coming, he set the emergency brake and motioned the riders over. Still mounted, they rolled the cycle to Nick's side of the truck.

"Hey," Nick said softly as the two men peered in through the window. They looked the same, except that Deadline's long brown hair had a few gray streaks in it, and Banjo's tanned cheeks looked like old leather. Both wore mirrored shades.

"Hey, yourself," Banjo said, grinning.

"Thanks for the help back there, buddy."

Banjo shrugged. "All in a day's work."

"By the way, I'd like you to meet Laura Rhodes," Nick said. Laura smiled at them. *God, she's pretty,* Nick thought, seeing her as his two old friends must. The man who ended up with Laura Rhodes would be one lucky son of a bitch. He wondered if there was any chance he would be that man.

"I'd like to thank you, too," Laura said. "Your performance was pretty impressive."

"That was nothing." Banjo inclined his head in Nick's direction. "You shoulda seen this guy in his prime. Nobody could touch him for accuracy. He could fling that ball peen hammer about—"

"Never mind," Nick said. "Listen, I have a favor."

"Sure. That's what we're here for. That and we might see a little of the city."

"Then this fits right in. I want you to look for my brother's car. It's a red MR-2. The license reads FST BUCK. If you find it, leave a message on my machine."

"Sure thing."

Nick glanced into his mirror again. Two cars were coming up behind him. "We'd better go. You guys are welcome to stay at the house. You know that."

"Yep," Banjo said, "but we ain't doing it." He raised his voice. "Thanks for the directions, buddy!" Then the two sped away down the street.

"They seem really nice," Laura said. "Have you kept in touch with them all these years?"

Nick shook his head, released the emergency brake and put on the right-turn signal. "But apparently life hasn't changed for them. I called the old number where they used to live. It's a converted warehouse in a crummy part of L.A. and Banjo was still there." He made the turn and started toward downtown. "They may seem nice to you, Laura, but you have to remember that these guys don't hold down a job. They don't pay their taxes, read to their kids at night, bring home flowers for their wives. They don't have wives, just 'old ladies.'"

"So did you have one, an 'old lady'?"

"Three."

"All at once?"

"No, not all at once! What sort of guy do you take me for?"

"Well, you paint this picture of a wild life, so I could imagine anything. Sex orgies, for example. And the way you affect women, it wouldn't be incomprehensible that you could keep three women—"

"That's quite enough." He frowned. "Every relationship I've had since I was fifteen has been monogamous, I'll have you know."

Laura looked amused. "You sound as if I've insulted you. Do you know how many men would brag about keeping three women on the string? Or boast about how far they could fling a ball peen hammer, Mr. Hammer?"

"Banjo has a big mouth," Nick muttered. He was almost regretting that he'd called the Vipers in, but he hadn't been able to think of any other way to guarantee their safety along the coast road. Without Laura in the truck he might have chanced it alone, but with her, he'd been mighty glad the Vipers had been on the job. He glanced at Laura. Her deep brown eyes were hidden behind dark glasses. She'd taken time to put on lipstick, probably while he was locking the house and putting up the garage door, and he had the urge to kiss that pink stuff away.

"When we go to the department store, would you do something for me?" she asked.

"What?"

"Put on a long wig. I want to see what you looked like as a Viper."

"Cut that out." He put on his meanest look, but she laughed even harder. He could only think of one way to make her quit laughing, and that would require both hands and a large bed. "Here's the bank," he said, swinging into a metered parking space. "Maybe you'd better stay in the truck. I'll just go in and draw out some money, act like that's my only purpose. I'll find out if anybody's stirred up over Lance not being there. If you come in with me, that'll cause more questions."

"Probably. Your idea sounds good to me."

"Lock up after I leave, and if you have any problems, honk the horn as long and loud as you can."

"Right."

He stepped out of the truck and watched her push the lock down. Then he waved and walked over to put some money in the meter. He glanced back one more time and she was watching him. He waved again, and she blew him a kiss. He fought the urge to yank her out of the truck and return that kiss a million times over. Dammit, she was really playing with fire.

Still, he couldn't help smiling as he walked into the bank. A wig. Lord Almighty. He had to admit that she had spunk. A man with a viper tattooed on his arm didn't intimidate her. Of course, if he had been able to dominate her, he wouldn't be falling in love with her now.

Falling in love? The words had slipped so easily through his mind, as if on a track already grooved for them. Love. It was an emotion he didn't indulge in lightly. Lust he'd readily acknowledge, would have to acknowledge, considering the activities he and Laura had engaged in the night before. Lust didn't usually hold such power over him, but he'd chalked that up to finally running across a woman who was his sexual equal. Maybe that wasn't quite the right explanation. Maybe love *had* somehow crept in, making plain old lust fizz and bubble like fine champagne. Maybe he was in worse trouble than he'd thought.

"Nick?"

He turned, remembering he had a mission in this building, a mission he'd nearly forgotten while he stood in a daze, thinking about Laura.

Lance's friend Sherry, the woman he'd called from Monterey, came toward him. She was a well-built blonde who only stood about five feet tall, even in heels. "How's Lance?" she asked.

He kept his tone neutral. "How do you mean?"

"I wondered if his stomach's better. I'm sure he's told you all about the food-poisoning incident."

"No." Nick thought fast. "I haven't been home yet. I thought I might find him here, since he didn't go to the seminar."

"Poor guy," Sherry said, making a sad face. "He called in first thing this morning and said he'd spent the night in some emergency room and was going home to recuperate. I said I'd come by after work to check on him, but he asked me not to because he just wanted to sleep."

"I see." Nick had always known Lance was clever. Scared as he was, he was covering his bases. He was hiding somewhere in the city, and as of this morning he'd been fine. "Then I'll try not to disturb him when I get home."

"I would have called you in Monterey, like you asked me to, except I was sure you'd have left by then. What were you doing down there, anyway? Carpentry work for some rich Monterey people, I hope."

"No, I was helping a friend whose car stalled down there."

"Oh, Nick, that's just like you, helping people out."

Sherry obviously knew nothing about the arrival of Laura Rhodes. Lance, for not very admirable reasons, hadn't told her about a girlfriend from New Mexico. Sherry was a decent girl. Nick wondered how Lance always managed to hoodwink such nice women into believing he really cared about them. "You know I never meddle in Lance's business, Sherry, but I can't help noticing . . . You two are getting kind of serious, aren't you?"

She blushed. "You mean like marriage serious?"

"Well, yes."

"I think we are, Nick. How would you feel about having me as a sister-in-law?"

"I'd love it," he answered truthfully, although he doubted Lance had any more intention of marrying Sherry than he had of marrying Laura. Lance had discovered that some women were more responsive sexually if they believed a man was heading toward the altar, that he loved them enough to make a lifetime commitment. Lance had used that vulnerability to his advantage at least twice, and at this moment Nick could strangle him for it.

"I'm glad you approve," Sherry said. "I know Lance thinks a lot of your opinion."

Not nearly enough, Nick thought. *But he will, if I have to sit on him until he listens.* "I guess I'd better get on up to the window," he said. "I came in for some spare cash."

"Oh, sure. See you, Nick. Tell Lance I said to get well real soon." Sherry hurried to her desk, which was only a few feet away from Lance's.

Nick wrote out a check for three hundred dollars and took it to the first available teller. He'd decided to treat Laura to her new clothes. They wouldn't be fancy; he couldn't afford designer labels any more than she could, but he had a feeling that wouldn't be a problem with Laura. He looked forward to the pleasure of buying her something.

The teller had just handed him the money in twenties when he heard the horn blast. Fear slammed into him. He should never have left her alone. Closing his fist around the bills, he sprinted toward the double glass doors.

9

LAURA HAD REACHED for the horn without thinking when she spotted the chubby man driving a green sedan. Then she wished she hadn't scared him away. The green car sped off into the traffic and she managed to get only part of the license-plate number.

Nick ran out of the bank, his face white with fear, and raced toward the truck. In that instant she realized that he cared about her, really cared. Her heart swelled with emotion. Laura was so overcome by her discovery that he had to beat on the window before she remembered to unlock his door and let him in.

"What happened?" He leaped into the truck and grabbed her. "Are you okay? Did anyone try to—?"

"The chubby man," she managed, although she was terribly distracted by Nick's worried face, so close to hers, his lips agonizingly near. She wanted to take him into her arms and never let go. "He drove by."

"Which way?" Nick released her and jammed some money into her hand. "Hold this. We'll try to catch him."

"That way. He's driving a green car," she said, pointing to their right. "But he's gone, Nick. I got part of the license, if that helps."

He put the truck into reverse. "A little, although we can't go to the police with it yet." He checked traffic and swerved the truck in a U-turn.

"Nick, is that legal here in the middle of the street?"

He began to laugh. "We're carrying a two-million-dollar stolen artifact in the air vent, and you're worried about a U-turn?"

"I keep forgetting the mask is in there."

"I wish I could. Keep your eyes peeled. Look down the side streets for any sign of your green car."

"I'm looking, but I'm sure he's gone, Nick. I shouldn't have honked the horn and scared him away. Maybe he'd have loitered around, and we could have caught him."

"Maybe he'd have tried something funny with you because I wasn't there," Nick said. "You did the right thing. You're sure it was him?"

"Positive. And another thing, he drove past us before, in Monterey, when we came out of the police station. I recognize the car now, and there was something familiar about the person in it back in Monterey, except it looked like a blond woman with a bad perm. I guess this time he gave up on the wig."

"Okay, so we know he's tailing us. I wonder if he followed us all the way from Monterey. Did you see a green car anywhere around on the drive up?"

It was Laura's turn to laugh. "Right. A guy with a gun was chasing us and trying to shoot out our tires, and a motorcycle gang wrecked the car and escorted us into the city. No, I didn't notice a green car, but that doesn't mean it wasn't there."

"Yeah, we were pretty busy."

"Listen, Nick, you might as well give up on finding that car. He's long gone." She turned from the window.

"Maybe. Just keep looking. I have another idea. Do you still have the address where Atkins was supposed to live?"

She rummaged in her purse with her free hand. "Yes," she said, extracting the slip of paper. "But he won't be there."

"I know. But let me see it." He took the paper and glanced at it. "Okay, let's drive over to that neighborhood and nose around."

"What did they say about Lance at the bank?"

"Sherry told me he called in sick. Said he was at some emergency room all night with food poisoning. He's supposed to be home recovering. I didn't tell her he wasn't."

"So he is in on this. I kept hoping something would turn up to show that he didn't know anything about the mask."

"He knew," Nick said grimly. "And now he's hiding out somewhere. I wish I could figure out the place."

"So do I." She held up the wad of money. "Incidentally, you might want this back."

He shook his head. "That's for your clothes."

"Wait a minute, Nick. I can't accept—"

"Yes, you can. I should have thought to empty your stuff out of the Cadillac into my truck, as a precaution. I knew something was going on. You didn't. So let me buy you a few things."

Curious now, Laura counted the bills in her hand. "Three hundred dollars' worth?"

"It's not as much as you think. You're not in Clovis anymore, Laura."

"Good of you to mention it," she said, tucking the money into her purse. She wouldn't spend it all on herself, but wasn't about to argue. "I never would have— Oh, look! The Golden Gate Bridge!"

Nick sighed. "You're not getting much of an introduction to the city. We should be driving over that bridge, meandering along Fisherman's Wharf, exploring Chinatown. I'm sorry, Laura."

"Oh, well. I'll be living here, so I'll have time to see everything."

"Still? After all that's happened, you'll look for a job and settle down here?"

"Of course." She studied him. "You're not getting rid of me, if that's what you wondered."

He stared straight ahead, but the lines around his mouth softened. "I never said I wanted to get rid of you, Laura."

She decided to let the statement pass, though she was tempted to probe further, to discover what he did want. The look on his face when he'd raced out of the bank had told her more than he might be willing to admit. She was in no hurry.

BENNY USED every side street he knew as he sped home. The woman had seen him; he was sure of that. He should have used another disguise, but he'd counted on

San Francisco being busy enough for him not to be recognized.

He used the automatic garage-door opener he'd installed himself to put his car away. His brother-in-law's Lincoln Continental was still parked in the street, where it had been when Benny got home this morning. The boss had said he didn't intend to use it and waste gas until Benny had something to go on in the search for Lance Hooper.

Benny walked into the kitchen, where a homemade chocolate cake sat on the counter. Erma was making meat loaf, while her brother lounged at the kitchen table, smoking and reading the afternoon paper. At least he hadn't put his boots on the table. Benny knew his wife didn't like anyone hanging around the kitchen when she was working. He walked over and gave her a kiss. She gave him a look.

"Want a beer, boss?" he asked, opening the refrigerator. "We can go watch TV in the living room."

His brother-in-law put down the paper and crunched out his cigarette. "I want to know what you found out. You've been gone the whole damned day, no telephone call, no nothing, and you offer me a beer and TV?"

Benny closed the refrigerator. "I couldn't find Lance Hooper's car anywhere. I waited around his house for a while, and finally his brother and the girl came home."

"Did they see you?"

"Not that time."

His brother-in-law struck his forehead with his palm. "I should have known better than to send you out. When *did* they see you?"

"She did, the woman. They went to the bank, the one where Lance Hooper works. His brother went in and she stayed in the car. I had to drive by, boss. The traffic was moving, and there wasn't a place to park, and she happened to be looking."

"How do you know she recognized you?"

"She blew the horn, real loud. Then he ran out of the bank."

"Oh, that's great, Benny. Just great. I suppose they followed you here. Are they outside now with a few squad cars? Maybe I should have that beer."

"Humphrey, don't you pick on Benny." The high-pitched voice caused them both to turn.

Benny grinned wryly. "It's okay, sweetheart. I'm used to it."

"I wouldn't pick on him if he'd stop being an imbecile," Humphrey said. Then he turned back to Benny. "So they went to the bank. I wonder what that means?"

"I don't know, boss. Maybe they—"

"Be quiet. I'm getting an idea." He stood and jerked his head toward the living room.

"You want to watch TV, boss?"

His brother-in-law groaned and walked into the other room, shaking his head. "No, you pea brain," he said in a low voice. "I don't want my sister to hear this. She shouldn't know too much."

"Oh."

"I figure this Nick guy probably knows where Lance is. So here's what we do. About ten tonight, when it's good and dark, we drive over to the house, make sure Nick and the girl are both there. Then we go to a phone booth and call, say we have a message from Lance. He wants to meet his brother, alone, down at the Wharf."

"He does?"

"No, you idiot! We just say that! Then we go back, kidnap the girl, and force the brother to tell us where Lance is, or else."

"Or else what?"

"Just 'or else.' Do I have to spell everything out to you?"

"Boss, I'm not killing nobody."

"I didn't say that, did I?"

"No, but . . ."

"It won't get to that point. Trust me, Benny. This will work, or my name's not Harold Atkins."

"It isn't."

"I know. Maybe I should get it changed. I liked being Harold Atkins. Liked that house, too."

"I can see why you'd like the house, boss, but why change your name? What's wrong with Humphrey Asenfelter?"

His brother-in-law sighed. "That's what my parents used to say. They weren't too bright, either."

"WOW!" LAURA SAID; they'd just pulled up in front of the house she'd once believed belonged to a man named Harold Atkins. "This reminds me of the sort of place Shakespeare might have lived in. Look at the leaded glass in the windows." The two-story house, white with dark wood detailing, seemed straight out of an Elizabethan play. A wide expanse of green lawn was broken by a flagstone walk that meandered up to a carved wooden door. A driveway at one side curved around to the back of the property, probably to a garage.

"Let's see if anyone's home." Nick got out of the truck.

Laura followed, breathing in the scent of the pine trees that formed a backdrop for the house. Several rosebushes next door added their perfume to the late-afternoon air. Laura wasn't nervous; the phone had been disconnected, so she was sure Atkins was long gone.

Nick used the brass knocker, a lion's head with a ring in its mouth. He knocked several times, paused and knocked again.

"Are you looking for the Thurstons?" a woman called from a neighboring yard.

"Yes," Nick called back.

"They're due back later this evening," the woman said. "Of course, they'll be suffering from jet lag, so you might want to check back in the morning, late."

Nick took Laura's hand and led her across the lawn. The warmth of his touch traveled up her arm and spread throughout her body. She forced herself to keep her grip around his fingers light, as if he hadn't just flipped the switch on her sensual impulses.

"That was quite a trip the Thurstons took," he commented.

"My goodness, yes." She wore a golfing cap in white eyelet and had on gardening gloves that looked as if they'd never touched dirt. She held a pair of stainless-steel clippers in one hand. Laura guessed she'd come out to cut a few roses for her dinner table. "They've been gone three entire months. I miss having Flo around. Their house sitter left this morning. He kept to himself. I never did even find out his name."

Neither did we, Laura thought. "I'll bet he enjoyed living in such beautiful surroundings for a while," she said out loud. Nick was brushing her palm with his thumb. She wondered if he was even conscious of doing it. She, however, was slowly turning into a walking bonfire as she remembered how that same lazy touch could bring her such pleasure.

"I wouldn't know if he enjoyed it or not," the woman said. "House-sitting seems like such an unsettled life to me. Lonely, you know? Of course, this man didn't seem to have many friends. The whole three months I only noticed two other cars there besides his Lincoln—a green car, one of those they make nowadays that could be any kind, and a little red one. I think my son said it was a Toyota."

Despite her resolution to stay relaxed, Laura clutched Nick's hand tighter. He squeezed back. The green car she'd expected. But Lance had been here, too. Plotting the smuggling of the stolen mask? She glanced at Nick, whose expression was as bland as if they'd been discussing the weather.

"We weren't sure exactly when the Thurstons would be back," Nick said, maintaining his firm hold on

Laura's hand. "We'll try again tomorrow, and thanks for the information."

"Oh, you're welcome. In case I see them, would you like to leave a message?"

"That's okay," Laura said. "I'm sure they'll have plenty on their minds, what with unpacking and everything."

"I'm sure they will." The woman smiled. "You seem like considerate young people. I hope to see you again sometime."

"That would be nice," Nick said. "Well, we'd better be going." He guided Laura back across the lawn and down the flagstone walkway. "I guess that just about puts a cap on it," he said after they were out of earshot of the neighbor. "Lance is in up to his neck."

"You're right." She didn't want to reach the truck. He'd probably let go of her hand then. "Boy, were you cool as a cucumber, Nick, acting as if we were close friends of those people—the Thurstons, was it?"

"The Thurstons." He smiled. "You weren't so bad yourself with that comment about not wanting to bother the Thurstons with a message."

"It was easy. That woman was just like my neighbors in Clovis, who keep track of everything that goes on across the hedge or across the street. I thought in a big city, in a rich area like this, it would be different."

"People aren't different, no matter where they live." Nick let go of her hand, as she'd known he would, and opened the truck door for her.

"Just like that, it's over," she said. She rubbed her arms to release her nervous energy. "You really are a cool character, Nick. Cooler than I am, that's for sure."

He narrowed his eyes. "What do you mean?"

"I thought you didn't want us to touch and stir up problems. I thought that's why you wanted us sleeping in separate rooms, but twice in the past hour you've violated that understanding. Once at the bank after I saw the chubby guy, and you were just holding my hand. Judging from your behavior, you're not affected, but as for me, I—"

"It's affected me." He shoved the offending hands into his pockets. "I acted instinctively, the first time because I was scared spitless for you, and the second because it seemed like the right way to put that neighbor at ease. Suspicious people don't run around holding each other's hands."

"I understand that. I'm only saying—"

"I know what you're saying." His eyes were bright with longing. "You don't want me to start something I don't intend to finish."

"Something like that." In reality she *wanted* him to start something—and finish it, as he had so beautifully, only this morning. The room in Monterey and their time there together seemed so far away.

"I'll try to think before I act next time."

"Fair enough." Her throat felt tight, but she managed a smile before turning and climbing into the truck. She heard his sharp intake of breath. He slammed the door and walked around to his side.

"I guess there's no doubt about Lance now," she said as he started the truck.

"That's right. I don't think Lance was over here picking up a deposit slip from his bank customer."

"No." Laura thought about the Lance she'd known in Clovis. True, he'd seemed a little on the reckless side, driving over the speed limit a lot and bragging about running up charges on his Visa Gold Card. At work he'd paid more attention to buttering up his superiors than attending to the papers piled on his desk. Laura had put it down to youthful exuberance and ambition. She wouldn't have guessed Lance capable of this sort of lawlessness.

"It's real, Laura," Nick said, breaking into her thoughts. "Lance is guilty of this crime, and he'll probably have to pay for that. I may, too, for concealing evidence. You can still take off, get away from here. I don't know how much longer I'll be able to say that, but I can say it now."

"Take off?" She turned to him. "And go where? Not Clovis, where I'd be bored to distraction, especially after what's happened to me in the past few days. Anywhere else I'd go I'd really be starting from scratch. Unless you're thinking of running?"

"Not on your life. If a patrol car stopped us right now and searched the truck, I'd confess. I'm not running from the law ever again. I *am* willing to buy a little more time, in case Lance shows up and I can talk him into going with me when I turn in the mask."

"When *we* turn in the mask."

"Oh, no. You're not going down to the police station. No need to fall on your sword, Laura."

"No need to be the big macho hero all alone, Nick," she said sharply. His stubborn independence was beginning to grate on her nerves.

"We'll settle that later. For now let's head to a department store and find you some clothes."

"Do we have time? What about Lance?"

"I've been thinking about that. We're probably wasting our time, running all over the city looking for him when the best thing might be to stay home and see if he comes to us. Banjo and Deadline will call there if they have any luck finding his car."

"Do you think he'll figure out that we have the mask?"

"I don't know. Eventually somebody will, but I don't think anybody knows for sure yet. That guy in the black Firebird had a hunch."

Laura shuddered as she remembered the rust-splotched car and the driver pointing his gun out the window. "The neighbor didn't mention a black Firebird coming by the house while Atkins was there."

"No, but we can't suppose she noticed everybody, especially if they arrived at three in the morning."

"I suppose . . ." Laura hoped what she was thinking wasn't true. "What if the man in the Firebird isn't working for Atkins?"

Nick sighed and straightened both arms, pushing slightly against the steering wheel with the heels of his hands. "Then this could get a whole lot more complicated than it already is."

"Do you have good locks at the house?"

"Yes. And the best alarm system on the market. I don't have much anyone could steal, but I've worked so hard on that house that I don't like the idea of anyone being in there uninvited."

"You have something someone could steal now."

Nick glanced at her. "Guess I do, at that."

"Nick, we can't risk going shopping for clothes. We can't leave the truck in some public parking lot while we wander around in a store."

"You have a point." He smacked his palm against the steering wheel. "Damn, but I wish we could do one thing together that's normal."

Laura said nothing, but smiled to herself.

"Besides that."

"How do you know what I was thinking? Maybe I was imagining that we could cook dinner together."

"Apparently you've forgotten the state of my kitchen."

"Oh. Right."

"Which means it's probably fast food from a drive-thru again. See what I mean? Here you are, your first night in one of the world's finest cities for eating out, and we'll have to grab burgers and fries or something."

She wanted to tell him that she'd eat soda crackers and drink tap water if she'd be sharing it with him. But she didn't. She reached into her purse. "If we're not buying clothes, I want to return this," she said, holding out the money he'd given her.

He shook his head. "This craziness won't last much longer. Tomorrow at the latest, it will all be over. Then you can get those clothes."

"With you?"

"That would be nice."

"No promises?"

He glanced at her but was silent.

Fear nestled in her stomach, a cold presence that she tried to push away. Finally she gave it voice. "Nick, you don't think this will turn out well for you, do you? You think you might end up in jail along with Lance."

"It could happen."

She stared out the window at the gathering dusk. "That's not right. You're only trying to protect your brother."

"Maybe it is right, Laura. I got off pretty easy back in my days with the Vipers. No jail time, a period of probation—that was it. It looks like I got off too easy. If I'd been really punished, if Lance had seen me suffer, he might not have considered smuggling a great way to make a few bucks."

"That's not necessarily true." Her single comment about Lance idolizing Nick had set off quite a reaction. She hadn't anticipated Nick's overdeveloped sense of responsibility toward Lance, or she'd never have said it. "I wish I'd kept my mouth shut," she muttered.

"No, I'm glad you spoke up. I might have put it all together too late. Now I stand a chance of being some real help to Lance, because I'm not judging him the way I would have before." He didn't look at her. "And in case I don't get another opportunity to say this, I think you're a terrific person. I'm a lucky guy to have known you, even for this short time."

"Will you stop spouting all these high-sounding sentiments?" She heard a trace of hysteria in her voice. "You sound as if they're already carrying you away in handcuffs."

He grimaced. "Sorry. You're right. No need to buy trouble yet. What'll it be, dinner with the Colonel or Ronald McDonald?"

"Chicken." *Which is what I am*, she thought. Despite her bravado earlier in the day, she'd finally admitted that she was scared—not for herself, but for Nick. If she thought she could persuade him to turn the mask over to the police right now, to claim that he'd just now got in from Monterey with it, she'd give the effort her damnedest. But she didn't kid herself. Nick was determined to give Lance plenty of time and not count the personal cost. She had to admire Nick's loyalty and sense of responsibility, but wished he wouldn't insist on being quite so noble.

10

THEY ARRIVED HOME with a bucket of Colonel Sanders' Kentucky Fried Chicken. The red light on the answering machine indicated two messages.

"One of these calls is Joanne's. I didn't take time to erase it," Nick said, setting the bucket upon his desk and switching on a desk lamp. "Let's hope the other call is from my dear brother."

"Let's hope." Laura listened again to the seductive note in Joanne's voice as Nick played the tape. She wondered if his assessment was right. Could Joanne's help be bought only with sexual favors? If so, Laura hoped he wouldn't ever have to finish the work on the lady's cabinets. Of course, he probably would, unless he ended up in jail. Of the two possibilities, Laura supposed Joanne and her cabinets was preferable.

The second caller wasn't Lance. Banjo's voice charged out of the microphone, almost as if he'd felt the need to intimidate the machine into submission. Laura guessed he wasn't much used to leaving messages on answering machines.

"We found your brother's car in a public lot down by the Wharf. Ticket says it's been there since 10:14 this morning. No sign of Lance. We've been everywhere in this city, even tapped into a few connections we have.

No luck. We'll keep trying." The message ended abruptly with a click and a dial tone.

"Where in hell *is* he?" Nick banged his hand against the side of the desk. "Dammit, but I wish that little twerp would show up."

"He'll call," Laura said. "Maybe he's tried and didn't want to leave a message. If I were hiding out, I'd be leery of making a recording that gave my whereabouts."

"I guess that makes sense." He glanced at her. "Want some coffee? It could be a long night."

"Sure."

"I'll go make some and bring it up." He started toward the stairs. "How do you like it?" he asked over his shoulder.

"Hot."

He paused. She could almost see the transition occurring in his thoughts. The one she'd intended. His body tensed and he gripped the newel post. He was remembering. Well, good. So was she.

"I'll be back," he said, his voice sounding hoarse.

"Good."

Laura watched the motion of his hips as he descended the stairs. She wanted him, wanted him with an elemental longing that startled her. She made a decision. She'd show Nick that their time together shouldn't be wasted, should instead be savored and embedded forever in their minds. Neither of them knew what lay ahead or when they might once again hold each other close.

Laura walked to the French doors and closed the drapes on the spectacular view of the city. Peeling off her T-shirt, she hurried into Nick's room, flicked on a light and opened his closet. Work clothes dominated the space, but at one end she found what she sought, a long-sleeved white dress shirt, silken soft. She nudged off her shoes and stripped off the rest of her clothes, tossing them onto his bed. She would have liked to leave a neater pile, but didn't have much time. Her body felt alive, tingling with knowledge of the outcome of her plans. He wouldn't be able to resist her. She knew him too well.

Taking the shirt off its hanger, she put it on. It fitted exactly as she'd wanted, the hem hanging to midthigh. She fastened the buttons, enjoying the whisper of the fabric against her bare breasts as she worked down to the bottom. Then she rolled the cuffs to her elbows and turned up the collar around her throat. A quick spray of cologne from her overnight bag, a finger combing of her hair, and she was ready. Her nervousness and anticipation increased when the aroma of coffee drifted up the stairs. Nick would be back very soon.

She returned to the study and considered the lighting. The desk lamp glared like the headlamps of a car. She bent the flexible neck of the lamp until the light reflected against the wall, muting the glow. Then she took a leg out of the bucket of chicken and carried it to the couch. By the time she heard Nick's tread on the stairs, she was reclining like Cleopatra on her barge, her bare legs crossed and propped on the couch while she nibbled at the chicken leg.

His pace slowed as he climbed the staircase. He must have noticed the lighting was different. When he appeared, holding a tray with mugs and a pot of coffee, she sent what she hoped was a meaningful look in his direction.

Even in the dim light she saw passion leap into his eyes, and her heart beat faster. His gaze swept over her, then returned to linger on the first fastened button of her shirt, where she knew the shadowed swell of the top of her breasts was visible. She toyed with the button with one hand. Then he focused on her mouth as she nibbled the rest of the chicken leg. She paced herself, using her teeth and tongue in ways that would remind him of what they'd shared, of what she'd discovered about pleasing a man—and saw tension build in him.

When she'd finished, she ran her tongue over her lips. His lips parted; his breathing grew shallow. She had him. Her heart thundered in her ears and an ache grew deep within her. She wanted to leap from the couch and fling herself into his arms, but that might break the spell she was weaving. She forced herself to move slowly, as if in a dance. She placed the bone upon a napkin and licked the crumbs from her fingers. He still didn't move.

Looking down, she brushed a stray crumb from the open lapel of the shirt. Then she unfastened the button that held the shirt closed and brought up her gaze slowly to lock with his. "Hungry?" she murmured.

He closed his eyes. His internal battle didn't last long. Before she'd drawn a complete breath he'd rid himself of the tray and crossed the room. "You're a devil," he groaned, pulling her from the couch to stand before him. "But I have to have you. I need you—need this...." Whatever else he might have said was obliterated by the meeting of their mouths—lips seeking, finding and rising to seek again, to find, to signal desire beyond the scope of words. She breathed in the scent of him, mingled with the aroma of the coffee on the desk. Her hands roamed his body, tugging his shirt away to run her fingers up his spine.

They were both gasping for breath when he pressed his mouth to her throat. The shirt she wore hung from one shoulder, exposing her breast to his searching hand. He squeezed, wringing a soft moan of passion—and triumph—from her. The shirt was still in his way, and he tugged at the next button. When it wouldn't give easily, he pulled harder, popping the buttons and tearing the material. She relished the frenzy she had created. To be loved with no restraint, to be sought as if no barrier could separate them, sent a white-hot current of desire through her.

At last the shirt was open; he stroked down her belly and tunneled through damp curls to the source of her throbbing need for him. She moaned against his neck as his fingers probed deep. She would have crumpled to the floor without his strong arm around her waist. She'd never known hunger like this before, hunger that left her shameless, giving herself up to his touch, his lips, his voice.

His voice rasped in her ear. "That's it. Let me hear you whimper, Laura. I don't care what happens when I'm loving you like this. Nothing else matters." He stroked her relentlessly. She gave him what he asked for, gave him—immersed in the magic rhythm of his touch—her final gift. He laughed exultantly and kissed her on the lips.

Then, while she still reeled with sensation, he guided her back to the couch and settled her there while he flung away his own clothes. She would have thought herself sated, so complete was the release brought by his caress. But as she watched his body emerge from the confining shirt and jeans, when she viewed the proud thrust of his erection when he stripped away his underwear, she ached anew.

He gazed down at her. "I've always been so sure of my control, my power over myself. With you I have none."

"I meant you to have none," she murmured. "I seduced you. This isn't your fault. I take all the blame."

"No." He scooped her into his arms and carried her toward the bedroom. "No blame," he whispered against her cheek. He laid her upon the striped comforter and stretched out beside her. "You made a promise with that performance," he said.

She understood. Kneeling over him, she touched him as intimately as he'd touched her, finally using her lips and tongue to wring moans from him that fueled her own desire.

At last he grasped her shoulders and laid her back onto the bed. "You asked where you belong," he said, moving over her and bracing his arms on either side of her head. He gazed deep into her eyes. "You belong here, in my arms. You match me, passion for passion. I was a fool to think anything mattered but this." He drove deep, and she rose to meet him.

"This is life, Laura!" he gasped.

"Yes." She rotated her hips to increase his pleasure.

"Ah, Laura." His breathing quickened. "You're everything I could want. Everything."

She'd thought to concentrate on satisfying *him*, but he knew how to move, where to press, what rhythm to take. Tension coiled within her, surprising in its intensity, and she could only hope he was following her in this quest for fulfillment. She dug her fingers into his buttocks and murmured his name in time with his thrusts. Then there was no turning back; he catapulted her once again to a shattering release. Moments later he shuddered and closed his eyes; ecstasy had overtaken him, too. Slowly he eased himself down to nestle his slick body against her breasts. His head rested in the curve of her shoulder.

"To hell with everything else," he murmured. "I love you, Laura."

Tears sprang to her eyes and she held him tight. "I love you, too."

"We didn't mean it to happen."

"No," she said, almost choking with emotion. "But we can't stop it now."

He sighed and stroked her hip. "I wouldn't even want to try."

NICK LOST TRACK of time. He felt as if he'd melted into her; surely she'd always carry traces of him, no matter where she went or how far away. For the first time in his life he thought seriously about marriage, about kids. He'd often wondered if he'd ever want his own. Now he had the answer. Only one woman could be the mother of those kids—the one lying with him tonight, breathing softly, her heart tapping out a quiet rhythm after the needs that had torn at them had been satisfied for a while.

An hour ago he'd never have admitted to himself that Laura mattered more than anyone else, even more than Lance. He had to admit it now. Lance came second. His little brother might be furious to discover that Nick and Laura were lovers, but Nick didn't intend to hide it anymore. As if he could. Hiding his love for Laura would be like trying to camouflage an elephant behind a potted palm.

No, Lance would have to take the news, just as he'd have to turn himself in, along with the mask. Nick realized he might end up in the same cell when that time came, and hated the idea of leaving Laura alone. He didn't doubt she'd manage; she was courageous and resourceful, two of the qualities he loved about her. He hated leaving her because it would hurt her...and him. Two days ago he hadn't yet felt her touch. Now he wondered if he could live without it.

When the telephone rang, his first emotion was resentment. Couldn't the world leave them alone just a little longer? He eased himself up with a mumbled apology, allowing himself one moment to gaze into her luminous brown eyes, then left the bedroom.

He answered the phone on the third ring. When he heard Lance's voice, he tightened his grip on the receiver and felt the edge of the desk bite into his other hand. "Where in hell are you?"

"The Saint Francis Hotel." Lance sounded hung over.

Nick tried to squelch his anger. He should have known his little brother wouldn't hide out in squalid surroundings. "What do you mean, in the Saint Francis? Are you in the bar or what?"

"In my room. Number 305. I need you to come over here, Nick. I need to talk to you."

"You booked a room at the Saint Francis?" Laura came up behind him and laid a soothing hand upon his arm; only then was he aware that he'd been shouting.

"Not under my own name. The desk clerk thinks I'm Richard J. Quick, from Portland. Get it? Rich Quick."

"I'll Rich Quick you, you crazy fool. Listen here, you—" He caught himself as Laura whispered to him to calm down. She was right. He'd planned to handle this differently. "I'll be right there." He glanced at her. "I'm bringing Laura."

"Don't do that, Nick," Lance said.

"I have to. I'm not leaving her here alone. We'll be there in— Just a minute, Lance." Nick covered the mouthpiece and glanced at Laura, who was tugging at his arm. "What's the matter?"

"I'll stay here," she said. "It's the logical thing to do. If you drive the truck, you'll have to leave it parked somewhere, and you can't afford to take a chance someone will see the truck and look for the mask. Leave it here with me."

"No. I'm much more worried about you than that mask. I don't care what it's worth. Besides, we can take the mask up to the hotel room with us, if that's a problem."

"Too risky," she insisted. "Besides, I don't think you should have the mask with you. You can tell Lance you have it, but I wouldn't tell him where it is. You don't know for sure what he'd do."

Nick considered that. She had a point. People could change pretty fast when a couple of million dollars were involved. He didn't know exactly what Lance would do, given that sort of temptation. His little brother hadn't shown himself to be of a particularly strong character up to now. "Lance, you still there?"

"Yeah. Listen, Nick, if you have to bring Laura, just don't come, okay? I'll work it out myself."

"Lance, wait a minute. Laura won't—"

"I don't want her here, okay?" Lance sounded on the verge of hysteria. "Just you. If it can't be that way, then forget it. Just forget it."

Nick jumped at the sound of the phone being slammed down. He held the receiver away and looked at it. "A little touchy, are we, Lance?"

Laura had gathered up his clothes while he'd been talking. She handed them to him. "Go talk to him, Nick. And leave the mask here."

He shook his head, but took the clothes.

"You said yourself the locks are good, and you have an excellent alarm system. I'll be fine."

"I don't like it." Yet he found himself dressing even while he rejected the idea of leaving her.

"If you don't go soon, he's liable to check out of the hotel and go somewhere else. You might never find him."

She could be right. For the next hour or so Lance would stay at the Saint Francis. If Nick didn't show up, he'd probably take off. No telling what would happen to the little jerk after that.

"How far away is the Saint Francis?" Laura asked.

"Twenty minutes." He propped one foot on the desk chair and tied one Reebok running shoe.

"That's not bad. If you make fast progress in talking Lance into coming home with you, you might be back in less than an hour."

"If I don't make fast progress, I'm leaving him there." He tied the other shoe. "I won't be gone longer than an hour, no matter what he decides. An hour is too long. And another thing. I haven't the foggiest idea where to hide the mask."

"I have."

A DARK BLUE LINCOLN stopped a block from the house just as the white Hooper Carpentry truck backed out of the driveway.

"He's leaving, boss, and we didn't even call him yet!"

"Be quiet. Can you tell if he's alone?"

Benny trained binoculars on the truck. "Looks like it. Where do you think he's going?"

"If I knew that I'd know what to do, knucklehead. He might be going to see that blasted brother of his. Then again, he might be heading to the store for a six-pack. One of us should follow him and the other one stay here and kidnap the girl. Except I don't want you driving this Lincoln, and I don't think you'd kidnap right, either."

"He's getting away, boss."

"That's right. That's because I've decided we go with the original plan. We'll kidnap the girl. After the way you said those two were going at it in the hotel room in Monterey, he'll be back. When he gets home, he'll find a note, saying that if he wants the girl back, he'd better tell us where his brother is. That way we still work everything out. See?"

"I always said you were the brains of this outfit, boss."

"Which is the one time you've been right. Come on. Let's find a way to get into that house."

NICK DROVE as fast as he dared through the hilly streets. His truck bottomed out a couple of times, and his tools jounced and rattled in the back, but he didn't care. Traffic was light, and he hoped there weren't any squad cars lurking along his route. His twenty-minute estimate for Laura's benefit had been calculated on the basis of a reasonable speed. If he drove the streets like Steve McQueen in *Bullitt* he might make it in ten. That left another ten to get back, and five to convince Lance that he should come home with him and go to the police in the morning.

Nick hadn't decided exactly when to tell his brother that he had something special going with Laura. Maybe on the way home, when the cab's doors were locked and Nick was driving too fast for Lance to jump out. But he wanted him to know before he walked into the house, before he saw Laura and perhaps thought of something stupid, like trying to kiss her hello. If Lance tried something like that, he'd have to deck him, which wouldn't be a good step toward mutual understanding.

He had his windows up against the night chill and his fog lights on. Despite the cold and fog, tourists walked the streets and taxis whipped through the traffic around Union Square. Nick checked for a green sedan or a black Firebird. He wished his truck wasn't such an obvious mark; its stark white color and the Hooper Carpentry sign on both cab doors identified it all too easily. He decided to park in an underground lot and walk to the Saint Francis.

A doorman in the costume of an English beefeater greeted him and raised his eyebrows just the slightest bit at Nick's nylon jacket and jeans. Most of the people in the lobby wore evening dress, but Nick proceeded inside as if they, not he, were out of place. He glanced around but saw nobody who looked suspicious, then headed for the elevator.

He rode up to the third floor, acknowledging that Lance had picked a good hiding place. Not many people would expect a young man without a large income to check into one of San Francisco's most prestigious hotels when he was on the run. But the move was perfectly logical for his little brother. Lance had bragged about getting a Visa Gold Card, thanks to a little creativity in his financial declaration. Nick should have expected him to use it—that was Lance's style.

He found the room and knocked. There were footsteps, then a pause; he imagined Lance peering through the peephole. At last the door opened and Lance pulled him inside.

"You're alone. That's good." His breath smelled of wine.

Nick saw an empty bottle in a bucket of water that had clearly once been ice. His brother wore a silk shirt and a fashionable pair of slacks. Both looked new, and exactly the right cut for Lance. He knew how to dress to show off his slender good looks. "Roughing it, I see," Nick said.

"I had to do something. Damn dog took a chunk out of my leg. Hurts like hell."

Nick stared at him. "You were in the wrecking yard?"

"Yeah, for all the good it did."

"Lance, I hope you didn't steal that car and kill those dogs. If so, we have a lot more to discuss than I thought."

"Steal it?" Lance lowered himself onto a chair with a grimace of pain. "Hell, no, I didn't steal it. What would I want with the car? And the dogs were fine. One of them came to before I got out." He eased up his pants leg to reveal a jagged, crusty wound on his calf. "As you can see."

Nick winced. The bite was red and swollen. "That should be looked at."

"Tell me about it. But first you have to help me with some other things."

Nick bristled at the tone of command. Then he realized Lance had always taken that tack with him. It was the response of a spoiled child. His stepmother and father had let Lance get away with it, too. Nick looked his brother in the eye. "I intend to help you."

Relief showed in Lance's eyes. "I knew you'd come through for me. Now first of all—"

"I have the mask."

"You?" Lance's jaw dropped. As he recovered himself, a smile spread across his face. "I don't know how you did it, but you just saved my life, just like that. You are something else, big brother. I owe you one."

Nick kept his gaze steady. He forced himself to remember that Lance had put Laura—all of them—in jeopardy because of his own childish greed. "You can repay me by turning yourself in, along with the mask."

Lance leaped to his feet. "You've gotta be crazy! Do you know what that thing is worth?"

"Roughly."

"Nick, think about it! Look, we don't even have to cut Atkins in on this. I know who the buyer is. He told me once, and I've made some careful inquiries. We can call him now, right here at the hotel, and arrange our own sale." Lance was excited. "Two million bucks, Nick, maybe more if we can squeeze it out of the guy. We'll take the money and go, head for Canada. Ever fancy yourself living in Vancouver, or maybe Banff, Lake Louise? Some beautiful country there, buddy."

Nick hadn't expected this to be easy, but was beginning to realize it might be impossible. "I like it just fine in San Francisco," he said.

"I don't know why. That jerk P. Delwood Chambers keeps blocking your contractor's license. Okay, here's another thought. We live in Canada awhile, keep on the move. Probably should until the commotion dies down a little. Then we come back, go somewhere else, like... I don't know... Hawaii. You'll get your license, no sweat, and have plenty of money to finance your business. Hooper Construction." Lance swept one palm through the air and glanced at Nick. "How does that sound?"

Nick gazed at his brother. The kid was smart. He knew which buttons to push. He'd fed Laura the line about making a new life in California, and she'd fallen right into his arms. He'd never intended to follow through with her, and probably didn't want to set Nick up in business, either. Not that Nick would want things to happen that way.

He thought about his stepmother. If she were alive, she would tell him to turn the mask over to the police and help Lance get out of the country for a while. Then she'd hit up his dad for some money to finance the getaway, and after huffing and puffing, he'd give in to Lance.

"I can see you're thinking it over," Lance said. "Come on, Hammer. Just you and me, buddy."

Adrenaline pumped through Nick's body and he clenched his fists. "You don't get it, do you? I joined that gang because I was a stupid kid looking for attention. I didn't do it for the thrills, and I certainly didn't do it for the money."

"Exactly." Lance pointed to his chest. "That's where I come in. You're streetwise, I'm not. But I know how to get money and you don't. Together we'll make it big. We'll have bucks, we'll have women, we'll have it all." He grinned. "So what are we waiting for? Let's go."

Nick took a deep breath. "No deal, little brother."

"No deal? What do you mean, no deal?" Nick saw a wary look come into Lance's eyes. "I get it. You're hoping to sell the mask yourself. You have it, so why split with anybody, right?"

"Wrong. I'm turning the mask over to the authorities. The only reason I've waited this long, and I may have made a big mistake in waiting, is to give you a chance to turn yourself in with it."

"No way."

"You really have no choice, Lance. You can't hide out in the Saint Francis forever, and I have a feeling some people will come looking for you. You're safer under police protection. You can testify against those guys and probably get your sentence reduced, since you don't have a record."

Lance's face grew tight with anger. He didn't look quite so handsome now. "Oh, I have a choice, all right. It's just that my big brother is acting like some judge and jury instead of a brother. I don't see where you have any room to come down on me, after the life you've led."

"You're right, I don't. But I also don't have the right to let you ruin your life, maybe even lose it, if I can stop that from happening."

"Where is the damn mask, anyway?"

Nick remained silent.

"You're not going to tell me, are you?" Lance's face grew red. "You're not going to tell me, you son of a bitch!" He lunged toward Nick, his fingers curved to fit around his brother's neck.

Nick caught his wrists and held him away. "Stop it!"

"Tell me!" Lance snarled. "Or so help me, I'll—"

"You're pitiful." Nick shoved Lance away. "Don't try that again," he said, when Lance made a move toward him.

Lance had apparently remembered that he was no physical match for his brother. He stood a few feet away and panted like a cornered beast.

"Look," Nick said. "Come back to the house with me. We'll get the mask and go down to the police station. I'll be with you the whole time. It's the only way, Lance."

"No."

"Use your intelligence. Somebody stole that Cadillac out of the yard, killing both guard dogs in the process. They didn't get the mask, because I had it. I don't know if the person was Atkins, his chubby friend, the guy in the black Firebird or all three. But if you have that mask, they're all coming after you, or the money you make from selling it. You wouldn't stand a chance."

"I would if you'd help me."

"I won't. Not like that." He glanced at his watch. He'd already been at the hotel too long. He needed to get back to Laura. "You have two minutes to decide. Then I'm leaving, with or without you, and I'm turning the mask over to the police."

11

LAURA HEARD A NOISE. She put down her coffee mug and the piece of chicken she'd been eating. The noise came again—a kind of irregular brushing sound at the front of the house. Her heart beat faster, and she leaned forward to listen. Nick had been gone about fifteen minutes, although it seemed like hours. She'd put on her sweat suit while he'd walked around the house, checking locks. Then he'd explained the alarm system. She'd tried to feel safe, but the moment his truck had pulled away, she'd wanted to race after him and hop into the cab.

She'd restrained herself; this plan made more sense. Between the locks and the alarm system, if anyone tried to get in she'd know it. The brushing sound came again. Maybe it was the limb of a tree scraping the wooden siding of the house. Except she didn't remember a tree in the front. She wished she'd put on her shoes, but didn't want to take the time now.

Getting up from the couch, she walked barefoot to the desk and switched off the light. If someone was out there, she didn't want them to know where she was. She continued into Nick's room and turned off the light there, too. Only one more remained, in the kitchen.

She crept down the stairs, putting each foot down slowly until she was certain the step wouldn't creak under her weight. Her heart hammered, and breathing grew more difficult. She tried to breathe evenly, silently; she didn't want someone to hear her gasping. She thought of the two dogs that had been killed in the wrecking yard, then tried to block out the image, to stop scaring herself. It was no use. She was scared.

The light from the kitchen spilled into the living room. She would be caught in it unless she was careful. The living-room windows were uncurtained, probably because Nick hadn't gotten around to that stage of his renovation. Laura crouched and used a chair and end table for concealment while she made her way to the kitchen. She crawled on hands and knees for the last five feet of the journey, reached up to the wall switch, and plunged the house into total darkness. She stayed on her knees and listened, straining to separate benign sounds from suspicious ones.

Perhaps what she'd heard was a cat, rubbing itself against the house as it prowled the front porch. Nick would laugh his head off if he came back now and found her crouching in the darkness, frightened out of her wits by an alley cat. Then she heard voices. Men's voices.

Something seemed to be stuck in her throat. Beads of sweat popped out on her upper lip, and she began to shake. She wasn't imagining this. Two men were outside the house, very close. She wanted to run, but wouldn't know where to go and didn't have shoes. She needed a weapon.

Crawling into the kitchen, she ran one hand along the bottom cupboards until she found a row of drawers. Slowly she eased the top one open and put her hand inside. Empty. The next one she tried was stuffed with dish towels, and the third contained booklets and slips of paper. She reached into the fourth drawer and touched a wooden handle. Stupid place for a cutlery drawer, she thought. Obviously not set up by someone used to working in a kitchen. A careful exploration revealed which instrument she wanted. She crawled back toward the living room, a knife with a long blade clutched in her right hand.

The living-room windows began less than three feet from the floor. Laura kept herself below that level and worked her way toward one of them. The voices came from the right-hand corner of the house, on the opposite side from the garage. If she peered over the sill she might be able to see them without them noticing her. She also might be able to make out their confusing mumble.

She heard someone panting and realized it was herself. She closed her mouth and struggled again to breathe normally. Nick had said the trip to the Saint Francis would take twenty minutes. He was already there. If his conversation with Lance was short, and she prayed it would be, he might be back in a half hour. It seemed like an eternity.

She reached the window and was very still. If she could hear what they were saying, she might know what to do. The windowsill, an inch from her nose, smelled of fresh paint. She tried to picture Nick on a sunny afternoon, working carefully with a paintbrush dipped in pale green. The image calmed her a little.

" . . . gone to bed," said a voice.

So they thought all the lights going out meant she'd decided to turn in. So far, so good.

"No, you pea brain," said one of the men, louder than before. Laura's scalp prickled. The voice belonged to Atkins. He mumbled something else, but all she could hear was the word "alarm." They'd figured that out. She wondered if they were trying to dismantle it, if it could be dismantled. She clutched the knife tighter and slowly lifted her head high enough to look out the window.

The two men were huddled together, and the light from a streetlamp didn't give her much help, but she could see that the taller of the two wore a cowboy hat, the same style she remembered seeing on Atkins. Despite her fear, she almost giggled. Someone would have to be a complete idiot to try and break into a house wearing a cowboy hat. Hadn't the guy heard of ski masks?

All at once she understood Atkins, knew he was a petty criminal who really didn't have his act together. She glanced down the street and saw the dark Lincoln Continental parked there. She realized that he used the car, the hat and the spider-trimmed boots to pretend he was some sort of big-shot crook. The only person who might believe him was the little chubby man next to him, the same one who had followed her up the coast. Lance might have been taken in for a while, but even he must know by now that he was dealing with bunglers.

Greater knowledge of her antagonists eased Laura's fears. Still, Atkins and his sidekick might accidentally dismantle the alarm system and get into the house. They wanted the mask, no doubt about that. It was probably the biggest haul they'd ever had, and would bring them enough to retire from the smuggling business. They could be desperate enough to be dangerous, and because they weren't accomplished professionals, they might panic. Laura pressed her lips together and faced the grim fact that her life was still in danger.

They moved around the house, out of sight, but she stayed at her post, listening. She looked at the knife in her hand and knew she wouldn't use it to keep them from getting the mask. She almost felt like putting the artifact on the front porch for them. That might solve all sorts of problems, including Lance's with the law.

Yet it would be an unworthy thing to do. Nick had risked so much to make this turn out right, and she couldn't just give the mask away because she was a little frightened of a couple of two-bit criminals. Besides, she was beginning to feel protective of the mask. She wanted scientists to unravel its mysteries, and that would never happen if Atkins had his way.

The men returned to their original position near the window, and she pressed her ear to the wall.

"You ring the doorbell," Atkins said clearly, "while I bring up the car. Tell her it's about that brother, Nick Hooper. That'll get her out here. Then I'll help you grab her."

"I don't know, boss. She's pretty smart."

"So am I."

Laura rolled her eyes. This might be easier than she thought. All she had to do was not answer the door.

"She'll fight us, boss."

"She's a woman, mush head. I can handle a woman."

Laura tightened her grip on the knife. How she longed to prove him wrong! But she'd stay right where she was until Nick came home.

"Okay, you got it?" Atkins said. "You get her to the door, I help you drag her into the car. Once Nick Hooper knows we have the girl, he'll tell us where Lance is, for sure."

Laura realized then that they didn't know she had the mask. They thought Lance had it, and wanted to kidnap her to find out where he was hiding. As long as she stayed inside the house, she had nothing to fear. Still, the idea that someone meant to haul her away and use her for ransom, even if the men seemed like mental rejects, made her stomach churn. She'd never been hunted before. Alarm systems and locks aside, it was a terrible feeling.

Atkins left to get the Lincoln, and the chubby man walked around the porch and climbed the steps. Laura could see his round face now, its expression uncertain. He didn't want to be doing this, she thought.

He waited until the dark car had been positioned opposite the walk, engine idling, lights off. Then he reached one pudgy finger toward the bell. Laura flinched when it rang loudly. The deep, melodious chime echoed through the house. It should have been a nice sound—she was sure Nick had chosen and installed that bell, taken pleasure in the richness of its tone. God, how she needed him here now. She waited, and the man pressed the bell again. And again.

She saw Atkins roll down the electric window on the Lincoln. "What's wrong?" he called.

"Not coming," the chubby man called back.

Muttering an oath, Atkins got out of the car and stormed up the walk. "Then we'll break in."

"But boss, the alarm!"

"Screw the alarm. We'll have her out of there and in the car before the police arrive, anyway. Come on. We'll break through the door."

Laura hadn't planned on that. She went numb as she watched them back away, both ready to charge the door. It was an old door. Maybe it would hold and maybe it wouldn't. She tried to think of a place where she could hide, but with two of them looking, they'd find her in a closet or under a bed. Probably they were right. They could drag her out and be gone before the police arrived. She could go into the garage, try to get out that door, but then—where?

She didn't know where, but it was the only plan she could come up with. She kept the knife and crept toward the kitchen, expecting any minute to hear the first thud against the front door.

Instead she heard the roar of a motorcycle. The heavenly sound of a motorcycle, coming, it seemed, right up to the front of the house. Someone began yelling, and she ran back to stare out the front window. Banjo had Atkins in a hammerlock, and his hat was on the ground. Deadline was holding up the pudgy man, letting his feet dangle. The little man's eyes bulged and he was clearly speechless with fright. Laura sagged against the window frame and gasped for breath. She was saved.

She turned off the alarm, twisted open the lock on the front door and flung it open. "Boy, am I glad you showed up!"

Banjo glanced at her right hand. "Looks like you were ready for them. Ever consider joining a gang?"

She looked at the knife still gripped tightly in her fist. "It was all I could find."

"You find real good."

"How did you happen to come by just now?"

"We didn't. We've been watching the house for a while. We saw the truck drive away without you in it." He reached down to pick up Atkins's hat and cram it over his bandanna. "Figured Nick might want us to keep an eye on the place."

"Good thing you figured it that way." Laura began to shake with relief. She was developing a great fondness for burly men in bandannas. They'd proved to be real friends. "I don't know how I'll ever be able to thank you."

"No need. Me and Deadline lost track of how many times Hammer saved our skins. And speakin' of our good buddy, when is he due back?"

"Any minute," Laura said, knowing Nick was probably breaking speed limits to return to her.

"That's good. I don't like leaving you alone, but we sort of need to cart this garbage away before we attract too much attention," Banjo said, pulling Atkins along by the neck. "If Hammer's due back, you'll be okay."

"What—what are you going to do with them?"

"I'll take this jerk on my bike, and let Deadline drive the other one in that fancy car."

Atkins groaned. "My car."

"Shut up," Banjo said, and tightened his grip.

"They should be turned in to the police," Laura said. "They're smugglers and potential kidnappers and—"

"We don't deal with cops," Banjo said, "but if you want, we'll put in an anonymous call, telling them where to find these two."

"Banjo, you won't . . ."

"Kill 'em? Nah. Not worth it. You'd better go back inside and lock up. All sorts of weird people running around tonight."

"I will. And . . . thanks. You guys are terrific."

"No problem. Give our greetings to Hammer." Banjo tied Atkins's hands and shoved him onto the bike.

"I might fall off!" Atkins complained.

"Now wouldn't that be too bad," Banjo said. With a wave at Laura, he was off down the street, the Lincoln following close behind. Laura had a feeling that when the police found Atkins and the chubby man, they wouldn't find the Lincoln. Banjo and Deadline would probably consider the car compensation for their trouble.

She closed the door and turned the dead bolt, then leaned against the door. They were gone. The smugglers who had been threatening hers and Nick's safety for two days had been whisked away by a pair of unlikely heroes. Now if Nick could just come home with Lance in tow, a remorseful, ready-to-make-amends Lance, perhaps they'd all get through this disaster in relatively good shape.

She flipped on the light in the kitchen and returned the knife to its drawer. Nick should arrive any minute, as she'd told Banjo and Deadline. Those two had saved the police some work. Maybe by the time Lance and Nick took the mask to the station, the police would already have been tipped off about Atkins and his sidekick. If Lance agreed to testify against them, he might get off without any jail time at all, just probation. After all, he'd never been in trouble before. Nick had, though, and that worried her.

She climbed the stairs and reached for the lamp on the desk. She turned it on—and cried out. A man was sitting on the couch facing her.

He smiled. "Everything all taken care of down there?" His voice was smooth, with the faint hint of a Spanish accent. His face was tanned, his hair dark, with a wave in it. He was almost handsome, except for a ragged scar from the side of his nose to the earlobe.

"Who are you?" she whispered.

"Doesn't matter."

"How did you get in? The alarm . . ." Then she remembered. In the jubilation following Banjo and Deadline's triumph, she'd forgotten to reset it. She glanced at the French doors. A pane had been cut from the one nearest the lock. With the alarm off, it had been easy to do.

"I was prepared to dismantle your boyfriend's cute little alarm, but in the end that circus out front saved me the trouble. I figured the alarm was off, so I swung up to the balcony and let myself in. It seems I owe those guys in the bandannas. Which is only fair, since they messed me up earlier today."

Laura's mouth went dry. "You're the man in the Firebird."

"I was the man in the Firebird," he corrected. "I was forced to commandeer another vehicle. Most annoying."

"If Atkins is your boss, they took him away. Any time now the police will—"

His laugh chilled her. "I don't have a boss."

Fear washed over her in a sickening wave. As a child she'd worried that she wouldn't be able to tell the difference between a gopher snake and a rattler. Her father had said, *When you see a rattlesnake, you'll know.* Her father was right.

If this was the man in the Firebird, then he probably had a gun. He was wearing a California Angels baseball jacket, roomy enough to hide a pistol underneath. Laura tried to control her terror.

"I'm sure you know why I'm here," he said. "So why don't you make this easy and hand over the mask?"

She wanted to do that, knew it was the prudent thing to do, but kept thinking that if she did, the evidence would be gone. Atkins and the chubby man would be arrested before morning, and they'd implicate Lance. Lance would have no way of proving that he'd meant to do the right thing. And worst of all, Nick would be dragged into it, since he'd transported the mask in his truck.

"It's foolish of you not to tell me where it is," the man said, drawing a gun. She'd been right. "I will find out and the sooner I do, the less angry I'll be. You can make things much easier on yourself by speaking up now."

She gripped the edge of the desk. "What makes you think I know where it is?"

He laughed, flashing his white teeth and stretching the scar across his face, widening the purplish zigzag. "Of course, you know. Once I discovered it had been taken from the car, I started narrowing down the possibilities."

"You killed those dogs."

He shrugged.

She thought about the butcher knife and wondered if she'd have had any chance if she'd kept it. Probably not. He'd shoot her before she reached him. But the way he shrugged, as if the lives of the dogs meant nothing, infuriated her. If she could think of a weapon, some way to throw him off guard . . .

"I thought maybe those two fools who'd managed to snatch the mask out from under me once had done it again, until my contacts assured me that the cowboy and his fat friend had no idea where the thing was. That left you and the carpenter or the carpenter's brother. I'm betting on you and the carpenter, but if I'm wrong, you'll take me to the brother, so I win in any case."

"I have no idea what you're talking about."

"I think you do." He got up from the couch and walked toward her. He was about six feet tall; from the easy way he walked and what he'd told her about his balcony stunt, she'd guess he was agile. She'd be no match for him physically.

"You can't kill me," she said, staring at the gun barrel that kept advancing toward her chest. "Then you'll never find the mask."

"You're right. I'm not going to shoot you unless you do something stupid and try to run." His dark eyes glittered.

"So why should I tell you?" She lifted her chin, determined not to look away from the evil in his gaze. "Then I'd be useless and you would certainly kill me. I'm better off keeping my mouth shut."

"You may change your mind about that." He reached out and slapped her hard across the face, making her stumble against the desk.

She gasped and tears of pain sprang to her eyes. No one had ever hit her like that. She held her hand to her cheek as it began to throb. He laughed, and she knew that he loved inflicting pain. Beating her would give him pleasure. He raised his hand again and she steeled herself for another blow.

It didn't come. He lowered his hand, kept the gun pointed at her and listened. She heard it, too. The garage door was rolling up. Nick was home.

"This may make things real easy," he said, grabbing her arm and dragging her across the room. "In fact, this may be absolutely perfect."

"Nick!" she shouted. "Go a—"

The intruder gripped her mouth so hard, she felt the imprint of his nails on her cheek. The smell of gasoline and cigarettes nearly made her gag.

The kitchen door banged open. "Laura?" She heard Nick come running through the house; he seemed to be leaping up the stairs. "Laura, are you—?" She saw him stop and drop into a semicrouch. His voice was low, almost an animal sound. "Let her go."

"As soon as you tell me where to find the mask," the other man said, pressing the gun barrel to her temple.

Despite her fear, Laura tried to shake her head, but he held her jaw in an iron grip.

"Sure, I'll tell you." Nick looked at Laura as if to reassure her.

Lance came up the stairs behind Nick. "What the hell is this?"

"He wants the mask," Nick said.

Laura saw the two brothers together for the first time and wondered how she could ever have imagined herself in love with Lance. Compared with Nick, he was no more than a boy.

Lance looked frightened. "Who are you?" he asked the stranger, who didn't respond. "Who is he, Nick?"

Nick kept his eyes trained on the man and flexed his hands. "I thought you might know."

"No." Lance's voice quivered. "Never seen him before."

"Lance, don't lie to me. If you know this guy—"

"He doesn't know me," the man interrupted. "He thinks, babe that he is, that the cowboy and the fat guy are the only ones who know about this business of smuggling Indian artifacts. Those two idiots are the dregs, the bottom rung on the ladder. Somehow they got lucky with the mask, but their luck just ran out. My client's offered to double the ante if I can produce the mask for him. Let us say I'm quite motivated to do so."

Lance sucked in his breath. "Double?"

Laura saw the greed in Lance's eyes. Funny how she'd never paid attention to the importance he placed on money, but now his priorities were clear. A man was pointing a gun at her head, while Lance was more concerned about how much the mask was worth. She glanced at Nick and knew he was trying to figure a way out of this so that no one would get hurt.

"You were playing around with losers," the man said to Lance. "Too bad you didn't hook into the right crowd."

"Listen," Lance said. "Maybe we can work something out. We'll give you the mask and—"

"Shut up, Lance," Nick said.

"Yes, you certainly will give me the mask," the intruder said, "or I'll blow this young lady's brains out."

"I said we'd give it to you," Nick snapped. He started toward the desk.

"Move real slow," the man said.

Nick slowed. He glanced at Laura and she could see the torment in his eyes. He was blaming himself for leaving her alone and putting her in danger. This must be torture for him.

"What'd you do, Nick, just stick it in a desk drawer?" Lance asked.

Nick didn't answer. Instead he picked up the bucket of fried chicken, took out the top three pieces, and pulled out a parcel.

"Unwrap it," the man said. "For all I know that's a package of chicken bones."

Nick peeled away the tissue and held up the plastic-wrapped mask for the man's inspection.

"Very nice."

Laura stared at the beautiful face and tried to absorb the serenity that flowed from it. She had a feeling that the calmer she was, the more power she would command. She concentrated hard on the mask.

"What a dumb place to hide it," Lance commented.

"No, it was very clever," the man said softly. "Almost in plain sight. If all of you had been gone, I might have torn the place apart looking for it and missed the bucket of chicken completely."

Laura thought she saw something in Nick's eyes. What was it? A communication? A warning?

"Nick, don't just hand the damn thing over," Lance said. "Let's bargain with the guy. Maybe we can work out a cut. I mean, fair is fair. We all helped get this thing up here. We deserve some of that four million."

Nick gave his brother a withering glance, then looked at the man. "Here it is. Lower that gun."

"Maybe I should just turn it on you instead." The man swiveled the barrel toward Nick. "You've been a lot of trouble to me. If you hadn't stepped in like the Lone Ranger and taken the mask out of the car, I wouldn't have had to go through any of this."

The mask's serenity had helped Laura to conquer her terror; she gazed over the barrel of the gun that was pointed directly at Nick's heart. She waited, heart racing, not daring to move. She didn't want to cause the man's restless finger to squeeze the trigger.

"So you want the mask?" Nick said, his gaze steady. "Here." He tossed it like a Frisbee, straight at the man's head. At the same moment, Laura bit hard into the fleshy part of his hand.

12

THE MASK SAILED through the air. Both Lance and the scar-faced man cried out. Laura tasted blood. His grip loosened and she spun away from her captor. She turned, just in time to see the man drop his gun in a frantic grab for the mask. He bobbled it once, flipping it into the air. Then he caught it in both hands, saving it from crashing to the floor, where it would have shattered into a million pieces.

Nick dived for the gun and had it pointed at the man before he recovered his balance. "Now," Nick said, taking aim. "We'll talk."

"You wouldn't shoot me," the man said, regaining some of his swagger. "You're not the kind used to guns. You're just a carpenter, a California yuppie like your brother there. You—"

The sharp report of the shot Nick fired made Laura's ears ring. The man wasn't hurt, but there was a blackened hole in the wall to the right of his head. His eyes widened and he took a step back.

Nick cocked the gun and aimed it again. "What was that you were saying?"

The man's confident grin faded. "All right, so maybe I was wrong."

"Maybe you were."

"If you shoot me, I might drop the mask. It could break."

"Ask me if I care."

"Nick, wait a minute," Lance said. "Think about this. The guy has a contact who will pay four million dollars for that piece of clay. Get him to tell us who it is. Make a deal. You're in the driver's seat now."

"Laura, come here a minute," Nick said. "Let Lance see that bruise turning purple on your face."

Laura walked toward Nick and stared at Lance with contempt.

He avoided her gaze, and she saw his cheeks flush. "Well, yeah, I'll admit the guy's a little rough around the edges, but once the deal is made, we don't have to see him again." He made a stab at regaining some of his bravado. "Be smart, big brother. I know you have a thing about Laura, and you don't like seeing her hurt, but four million dollars buys a lot of cold compresses."

Nick's jaw tightened. "If I didn't have something more important to do right now, I'd knock your teeth in for that remark."

Laura turned to Nick. She'd just realized what Lance's statement meant. "You told him about us, didn't you?"

Nick kept his eyes on the man standing across the room. "Yes. It seemed important at the time."

Warmth surged through her. Nick had been willing to declare his love and take his chances on how Lance would react. He'd made his choice, and she'd been chosen. It was more than she had dared to hope for.

"To my surprise, losing his girlfriend didn't seem to break my little brother up too much," Nick continued. "He was more worried about the whereabouts of the mask, and whether he could still somehow wrangle the money from the deal."

"That's not fair, Nick," Lance protested. "You—"

"Oh, it's fair, all right. You just proved my point. You're willing to deal with a man who brutally struck a woman you supposedly care about. You're not good enough to clean Laura's shoes."

"Cut it out, Nick." Lance sounded petulant now.

"You're right, we've talked about this enough. It's time to tie this jerk up and take him and you down to the police station, along with the mask."

"Don't do it, Lance," the scar-faced man said. "Be smart. Take that gun away from your brother, and you and I will make a deal. Obviously he and this girl aren't ready for the big time, but I can see you are."

"Don't try it, Lance," Nick said. "Trust that guy and you're a dead man. Laura, there's a roll of duct tape in the bottom left drawer of my desk. Get it and tape that guy's hands and feet together. Make it tight."

Laura found the tape and approached the man with caution. The closer she got, the more she realized that she would always associate the combined smell of gasoline and cigarettes with this man and with her fear.

"Give her the mask," Nick told the scar-faced man.

Leering, the man handed her the mask. "You're making a bad bargain, honey."

"Cut the conversation," Nick said.

Laura handed the mask to Nick. Then she returned, trying not to breathe too deeply. "Turn around," she said.

He held his arms limply at his sides; she gritted her teeth, brought his wrists together, and wound them with the silver tape. Any contact was repulsive, but she knew she had to do it.

"Sit down," Laura told the man. He lowered himself to the couch and she wrapped his ankles. She hated even the sound of his breathing. She didn't look into his face. She finished, took back the roll of tape and put it on top of the desk. She returned to stand beside Nick.

He clearly didn't trust Lance, who was lurking by the stairs, apparently too cowardly to make a move, yet not quite willing to accept his fate.

"Now let's call the police," Nick said. "I'd hoped to go down to the station with Lance and the mask, but this guy complicates things. Better if they come here."

Laura started for the telephone.

"No!" Lance lunged for the phone and grabbed it from the desk, breaking the cord.

Nick glanced at Laura. "Hold the gun on that guy." He thrust the weapon into her hands. She positioned herself to see both Nick and Lance while she kept the gun pointed at the man on the couch. She'd never held a gun, never fired one, but she'd fire this one if she had to. Gladly.

"Nick, give me the mask," Lance pleaded. "The mask and a head start, that's all I ask. You can tell the police anything you want. Just let me make contact with the buyer and get away."

"No deal." Nick laid the mask upon the desk and started toward his brother. "You're staying here, little brother. It's your only chance, whether you believe that or not."

"No!" Lance shrieked and hurled the phone at his brother.

Nick's reaction was too slow. The telephone grazed his temple, making him stagger.

"Nick!" Laura cried.

"Just hold the gun on that guy," Nick said through clenched teeth as he gripped the banister and hurled himself down the stairs after Lance.

She heard Lance's yell, then a thud. Nick must have tackled him at the foot of the stairs. She couldn't see them, but knew from the panting and scuffling noises that they were fighting. Bone connected with bone as someone's fist landed on someone's jaw. There was another thud, then more scuffling.

"Untie me and I'll make you a rich woman," the man said. "We're alone with the mask, and those two are very busy. Come away with me. We'll leave by the balcony, just like I came in. My car's close by."

Laura's jaw ached where the man had hit her. "Sure," she said. "I'll come away with you. I love getting biffed around." She listened to the noises downstairs. She thought Nick could have won easily if he hadn't been dazed by the flying telephone. He'd reacted slowly because he hadn't expected it, hadn't believed his brother would deliberately harm him.

"That little slap was a misunderstanding, sweet lady," the man continued. "I'll make it all up to you. Four million dollars. Who can turn away from that?"

"I can," she said.

There was another thud and someone moaned. The scuffling stopped, and footsteps started up the stairs. "All right, Laura," Lance said. "Give me the gun."

She watched in horror. He was pulling himself toward her, holding on to the banister for support. His nose was bloody, his clothes were askew, but he was clearly the victor, and Nick... "Where is he?" she whispered.

"He'll be all right in a little while." He staggered once and righted himself. "He shouldn't leave his tools lying around like that."

Rage threatened to destroy Laura's concentration. She remembered the carpenter's level that Nick had found in Lance's bedroom and left at the foot of the stairs. Obviously Lance had used it as a weapon. Slowly she swiveled and trained the gun on him.

Lance blinked. "Hey, what's this?"

"You don't deserve a brother like Nick, you slimy, repulsive—"

"Just give me the gun, Laura."

"No."

"Come on, Laura. That hoodlum over there is one thing, but this is Lance, your old pal. You wouldn't shoot me." He managed a smile. "Remember the times we used to have, Laura? Good times."

"Stay away, Lance." The gun quivered in her hand. He was right. She could shoot the man with the scar in a minute. Lance Hooper was another matter altogether. But he'd hurt Nick. Nick was down there, maybe unconscious, needing a doctor. Her hand steadied. Her voice calmed. "Come one step closer and I'll shoot you," she said, looking straight into his eyes.

"I'd believe her if I were you," Nick said.

She looked beyond Lance and saw Nick, dazed and leaning against the newel post. His forehead was bleeding where the telephone had caught him, and he had another bloody gash on the side of his head from his encounter with the level.

"She's not the little small-town girl you thought you left behind in Clovis, Lance," Nick said. "She's graduated to the big time, and in a hurry, too. She's one hell of a woman, and if she says she'll shoot you, she'll damn well do it. She's not nearly as gullible as I am, little brother."

Lance hesitated.

Laura decided he wouldn't try to get the gun away from her now. "Nick, can you make it back downstairs to call the police?" Laura asked.

"Sure. Looks like you have things under control here."

"I do." She glared at Lance and motioned with the gun. "Get over next to Scarface," she said.

Lance moved slowly, edging over to the couch. "Nick's right," he said, looking wary. "You've changed a lot."

"Too bad you haven't, Lance," she said.

THE POLICE CAME. Lance announced that it had been his idea to call them and turn the mask over to the authorities. Laura opened her mouth to contradict him, but Nick silenced her with a shake of his head.

The police had brought two squad cars and took all four of them to the police station. It was a busy place, much busier than the Monterey station had been. Exhaustion kept Laura from making much sense of what was happening, but she did hear that the scarred man's last name was Robles, and saw that the police seemed to recognize him.

Laura was the last of the four to be taken away for questioning, which gave her a chance to observe what happened when a curator from the museum came down to identify the mask. Laura had never in her life seen a person as happy as the archaeologist when he glimpsed the mask.

"You have no idea," he said, touching it with reverence. "A ceremonial artifact like this will be the crowning touch of the museum's ancient-cultures exhibit. And think of how this will expand our knowledge of Anasazi rituals! Their ways are still so mysterious to us. We know so little, and now this is discovered, so very different from anything we've unearthed so far. To think we almost lost the chance to study it. I'm overwhelmed." He sighed with pleasure.

Laura decided she'd keep close tabs on the research surrounding the mask. Someday she'd like to know if the sensations and images she'd experienced when she first saw the newspaper picture had any basis in historic fact. She remembered how the mask had filled her with courage when she'd been held at gunpoint. The mask was more than an old piece of clay, *much more.*

Soon after the curator had left to alert his colleagues of the mask's safe recovery, Laura was questioned about her part in the smuggling attempt. She told everything as it had happened and emphasized Nick's desire to protect his younger brother from harm. She hoped it would help. She asked about the gashes in Nick's head and was told they had been attended to.

Finally she was told she would not be arrested and that she could leave. Since she had no transportation of her own, a patrol car would escort her. "I'll wait for Nick," she said.

"I'm sorry," the officer replied. "Mr. Hooper will be detained along with his brother."

"So he has been arrested?" Laura's worst fear was confirmed when the man nodded. "But that's not fair!"

"I'm sorry," the officer said again. "I'll call for a patrolman to take you home."

"Can I see him?"

"Tomorrow. You can see him tomorrow."

DURING THE RIDE Laura fumed about injustice and castigated Lance Hooper. Greedy, selfish Lance. Laura no longer believed that Nick owed the creep anything at all. If Lance had used Nick as a role model, he'd missed several important ingredients like loyalty, integrity and compassion.

No, Lance was responsible for himself now. Nick had given him a number of chances to correct the mistake he'd made when he linked up with the smuggling operation. Lance hadn't wanted to be saved. Laura suspected he would have sacrificed both his brother and her if he could have somehow gotten his hands on the four million dollars Robles had dangled in front of him.

The patrol car stopped in front of Nick's house and Laura started to get out. Then she paused. "I don't have a key."

"Yes, you do," the officer said. He picked up an envelope lying on the seat between them. "Mr. Hooper asked that we give these to you."

Laura opened the envelope and took out the set of keys. A small silver hammer dangled from the chain. Tears pricked at her eyes.

"I'll come in with you," the officer said. "We'll close up that hole in the French door and make sure you have the alarm system turned on."

"I'm not afraid," Laura said. "Just make sure you put out plenty of police bulletins saying you guys have the mask, and nobody will care about me."

"I'm sure that's been done. There was a search going on throughout the country for that one—most valuable artifact stolen in a long time, the archaeologists said."

"Then the person who recovered it should be given some credit," Laura mumbled.

"What was that, ma'am?"

"Never mind." She sighed. "Let's go in the house."

Once they were inside, the policeman insisted on nailing a piece of board over the hole in the French door. Laura winced at the pounding of the hammer, knowing that the man was damaging Nick's door. Nick would have been able to fit something perfectly into the opening until morning, when he could have replaced the glass himself. But Nick was in jail.

Laura waited until the officer left, then went through Nick's Rolodex. She found a number for a lawyer named Jeperson. Carrying the Rolodex with her, she went downstairs to call Jeperson. As she dialed, her glance lingered on the cutlery drawer. So much had happened in such a short time.

Jeperson answered on the second ring. He sounded young and very much awake. "He just called me," he said. "Don't worry. I think we'll be able to get him out pretty soon."

"I want him out now," Laura said.

"He'll be arraigned tomorrow and the judge will set the bail. Considering the value of that mask, it could be pretty high, but if you can raise a substantial amount by then . . ."

Laura's spirits sank. "I'll see what I can do. What time's the arraignment? I'd like to be there so I can—"

"Uh, he mentioned that to me, Ms. Rhodes. He doesn't want you there."

"That's ridiculous! He may not want me, but I'll be there, nevertheless. You can tell him that."

Jeperson cleared his throat. "I, umm, sort of promised him I'd keep you away. He said that environment is no place for you. He was very specific. I think he mentioned something about firing me if I can't convince you to stay home."

Laura sighed. "Stubborn as always. Okay. We'll play it his way. Will you call me when the bail is set?"

"I can do that much. He didn't say anything about that. I'll be trying to raise some funds myself. I would use my own resources, except that I just started my practice, and my wife's expecting, and—"

"I understand," Laura said. "But maybe we can find someone else."

Jeperson wished her luck and she hung up. She hesitated only a moment, then flipped the Rolodex to find Joanne's number. A man, a very sleepy and irritated man, answered. Laura asked for Joanne and said it was urgent. Finally she heard Joanne's husky voice, made even throatier from sleep. Laura told Nick's story while Joanne listened silently.

"He'll need bail money tomorrow. He doesn't belong in jail," Laura finished. "I don't know anyone else in town but you, and I don't really know you. But I thought, considering that you think Nick is such a good carpenter . . ." Laura wondered what she'd just done. If Joanne agreed to bail Nick out, she might expect payment, payment of a sort other than monetary.

"It's a sad story, but I don't see why I should help," Joanne said.

"Because I don't know anyone else to call."

"Then I guess he'll just have to stay down there. Sorry." Joanne hung up.

Laura stared at the phone. She banged the wall as hard as she could with her fist and began to cry. Dammit, she should never have left New Mexico! Yet even in her despair, she knew that it had been the right decision. She'd figure some way out of this mess, but how? She banged the wall again. She felt so helpless, so alone. Damn Lance Hooper for being such a rat, and damn Joanne for being so coldhearted! She sobbed until she had no sobs left.

Then she leaned her forehead against the wall and tried to think, but was too tired to come up with other solutions. Finally she turned off the kitchen light and wandered upstairs to Nick's room. She lay across his comforter and felt the tears return as she remembered how Nick had loved her here only hours before. She fought back the tears and closed her eyes.

She awoke to the ringing of the telephone in the kitchen. She blinked in the sunlight, grabbed the small bedside alarm clock and discovered it was almost noon. Jeperson could be calling her about the bail. She stumbled down the stairs and picked up the receiver.

"Did I wake you?" Joanne's husky voice boomed into Laura's ear. "So sorry. Tit for tat. Listen, I've changed my mind."

"You'll do it?" Laura came instantly awake.

"Yes, and Lord knows why. No, I do know why. Nick's probably told you all about me and how I've tried to get him into bed. Yet you had the guts to call me and ask for help because I was the only person you knew of in this town with money. You must care a lot about the guy."

Laura swallowed. "I do."

"Then give me his lawyer's number. I'll see what I can do."

The Rolodex was still on the kitchen counter. She grabbed it and reeled off the number. "I'll never forget this, Joanne," she said. "I really mean that. I'll—"

"Never mind all that. If you get too sweet on me I might get nauseated. You just sit tight and I'll try to get your lover boy free." Joanne hung up.

THE PHONE WAS SILENT until five that afternoon, by which time Laura was a nervous wreck. She prayed the caller would be Nick and raced for the kitchen.

Joanne's voice greeted her instead. "He won't come out."

"What?" Laura blinked, not believing what she was hearing.

"Lover boy. I posted bail and he refused to leave. I even told him there were no strings attached. He still wouldn't come out."

"I don't understand." Laura tried to make sense of it. Nick had a chance to leave the jail, and he'd refused?

"That's not all. He told me to give you a message."

"A message?" Her stomach twisted. She wasn't going to like this message.

"Yes. He said the truck keys are on the ring you have, the one with the hammer on it. He wants you to use the truck to find a job and an apartment. Get out on your own. To use his exact words, he said, 'Tell her I'm cutting her loose.'"

Stunned by the unexpected harshness of Nick's directive, Laura gripped the phone. "That's it? He didn't say anything more about me?"

"That's it. And if you want my advice, honey, I'd do just what he says." Joanne lowered her voice. "Nick Hooper's a lone wolf and a heartbreaker. Don't waste your time."

Was she dreaming this phone call? Laura hoped she was. Nick *loved* her. He'd risked telling Lance about them and jeopardizing Lance's cooperation. He'd been willing to sacrifice a four-million-dollar mask to keep her safe. Now he was telling her to bug off? It didn't make sense.

"Laura, you still there?" Joanne asked.

"Yes," Laura replied. "Thanks for going down there. I really don't understand Nick's behavior, but I appreciate what you tried to do."

"Oh, well. Keeps my life interesting. Guess I'll have to find a new carpenter, though, if Nick's decided to be some sort of martyr. I don't suppose you know any— No, that's right, you don't know anybody in town except the Hooper brothers. And me."

"That's right. Well, thanks for everything, Joanne." Dazed and confused, Laura started to hang up the phone.

"Hold on a minute." Joanne's husky voice called her back. "It's tough to job hunt if you don't know anyone in town. What's your field?"

"Banking. I was going to use Lance and his contacts, but . . ."

"Not such a good idea right now. Look, my husband knows quite a few prominent business people. Come over for dinner tonight and bring your résumé. He should be able to help."

Laura felt embarrassed after all the nasty things she'd thought about this woman. "Really, that's not necessary. I'll just go out on my own tomorrow."

"My God, what have we here, a female version of Nick Hooper? I assumed when you called me for help that you weren't as pigheaded as Nick."

Laura started to reply, but Joanne barreled on.

"No strings attached to this, either, Laura. Come on over and let Roger help out. Don't be so damned independent. Be here at six. That gives you at least a half hour to get ready. Dress casual." Joanne hung up.

Laura replaced the receiver and pressed her fingers to her temples. She was nurturing a granddaddy of a headache after this latest disaster. The past few days had been a roller coaster of emotions, but this last jolt had been the worst of all, the steepest drop. Nick was cutting her loose. Cutting out her heart was more like it. His behavior didn't seem like the Nick who'd loved her so passionately, but how well did she really know him? Perhaps within the confines of a jail Nick Hooper had once again become Hammer, member of the Vipers. Maybe his rebel side had reasserted itself, and there was no room in that kind of a life for someone like her.

Maybe she should go back to New Mexico, where she belonged. Maybe . . . No, by God! She wouldn't give up!

She whirled and raced up the stairs. She would go to Joanne's, get that job, find an apartment. And she wouldn't give up on Nick, either. She loved him. Laura thought of the mask. That power wasn't gone. She'd use it to fight for Nick. Somehow, someday, he would be hers.

13

WITH THE HELP of Joanne's husband, Laura had a job by five the next afternoon. She was scheduled to start the following day. Setting up the job wasn't the hard part of carrying out Nick's directions. She'd been planning to find work, anyway. But she dreaded looking for an apartment. Once she left Nick's house, she would no longer have a physical connection with him. Living among his things, admiring his remodeling, sleeping in his bed—all of it had given her more hope that he'd contact her and tell her he hadn't meant what he'd said to Joanne.

Nevertheless, she'd bought a newspaper so that she could look through the apartment ads. But all day, as she'd shopped for business clothes, she'd left the newspaper folded beside her on the seat of Nick's truck.

By evening she had the hang of maneuvering the truck through the maze of San Francisco traffic. After the job was settled, she realized she was free to go anywhere she wanted and had wheels to do so. She decided to drive across the Golden Gate Bridge.

She joined the stream of cars, trucks and buses crossing the bridge into the lush landscape of southern Marin County. She relished every moment of the trip—

the buzz of the truck's tires when they touched the bridge, the soaring, red-orange span curving above her, the supports flashing by, and below her the sparkling waters of San Francisco Bay. For the first time she felt really a part of this city she'd dreamed of for so long.

Once across the bridge she pulled into a parking area and stopped the truck. The wind tugged at her hair as she stepped out, still dressed in the outfit she'd worn for her interviews, a green-checked suit and ivory blouse. She'd told herself the color had nothing to do with her observation that Nick seemed to like green.

The wind was cold, whipping up whitecaps on the Bay; pleasure boats scurried for their moorings, while large freighters plowed through on their way to the Pacific. If the smugglers had had their way, the mask would be on its way to the Orient by now, perhaps stowed in one of those cargo ships.

Laura was glad the mask would be displayed in a public museum. She felt proud of whatever part she'd played in keeping it safe for future generations. Nick should feel proud, too. Laura pulled the suit jacket tighter around her and leaned against the hood of the truck, still warm from the engine.

A few clouds drifted on the horizon, but none of them marred the brilliance of the sun as it touched the skyline with gold. San Francisco lay spread before her like a magical city in a fairy tale. Laura thought that if she'd had a choice, she would have wanted to enter the city first from this direction. Perhaps one day she'd live in Marin County and drive across the Golden Gate Bridge into the city every day.

She'd gone through a lot to get here, more than she'd ever imagined possible four short days ago. Her dreams involving Lance had gone up in smoke, but in the process she'd learned the power of real love, the kind she had for Nick. After meeting Nick and working with him to rescue the mask, and falling in love with him, she could never settle for anything less.

Her existence in Clovis had lacked drive and purpose. Her parents wouldn't understand that, and she could see now that for them eastern New Mexico was a wonderful place to be in. But living in San Francisco was an integral part of her decision to take charge of her life. She craved the city's excitement, the crisp ocean breeze against her skin, the scent of pine trees. Perhaps she'd always been free to live the way she chose, but the sight of the Golden Gate Bridge would remind her every day from now on, that she, and no one else, was the architect of her future.

She would make it here—she knew that without any doubt. She only wished she could share the triumph she felt with the one person who would understand. Yet he'd shut her out. She could guess at his reasons, but her guesses might also be wrong.

His recent arrest, no matter how short its duration, could end forever his dream of becoming a licensed contractor here. Nick might well believe that she shouldn't settle for someone who couldn't control his own future any better than that.

Then there was the matter of his leaving her alone with the mask. She'd talked him into it, and it had seemed like the only way, but neither of them had anticipated a criminal like Robles showing up. Still she believed that Nick blamed himself for putting her in danger, that his cursed sense of responsibility had made him feel unworthy of her.

Laura could accept those reasons, but in her blackest moments thought of others. What if Nick had been carried away by the emotions of their shared experiences and now realized he didn't want a permanent commitment, that he regretted his declarations of love? Joanne had called him a lone wolf. Maybe he'd decided to continue that life-style.

A single cloud eased over the sun, throwing the city into shadow. Uttering a sigh of resignation, Laura returned to the cab of the truck. Now was as good a time as any to look through the apartment ads. Then she could inspect a few on her way home. Home. No, she corrected herself, it wasn't home. It was Nick's house.

She climbed into the cab and unfolded the newspaper. She'd started to discard the front section when she noticed a story about the mask. A picture showed a beaming group of people identified as the museum's board of directors. One name leaped out at Laura. There, two from the left, was P. Delwood Chambers. If she wanted to fight for Nick, here was her weapon.

NICK RODE THROUGH San Francisco in his lawyer's Honda Civic the next evening, amazed how the buildings and even the people seemed to glow. It was either a weird trick of the sunset or a function of his new ability to appreciate freedom. "I still don't quite understand why the charges against me were dropped," he said, turning toward Jeperson.

"Don't ask too many questions is the word I got," Jeperson said, pushing up his glasses on his nose. "Somebody on the museum board found out about your role in getting the mask back. They have some clout, apparently, and the charges were dropped against you. Not against your brother or Robles or the other two they picked up. But you're a free man as long as you stay around to answer questions."

"I'll do that. I'd still like the full story about how Atkins—"

"You mean Humphrey Asenfelter?"

"Yeah, and the chubby one. I'd still like to know what happened with them. You said the police got a tip that they were tied up in the Japanese Tea Gardens?"

"That's right. So far they haven't told how they got there, either."

"Interesting." Nick thought he knew who had tied the two crooks up and phoned in an anonymous tip, but he'd have to call L.A. to make sure. He smiled. Banjo and Deadline were all right. He was a little amazed that they'd demonstrate such loyalty after all these years. Maybe everything about his gang years hadn't been terrible, if it could forge friendships like that. He'd go see them soon and thank them for saving his butt and taking care of Laura. Laura . . . Pain twisted in his midsection.

"You'll probably have to testify against your brother when the time comes," Jeperson said.

Nick sighed. He'd had many long hours to think about Lance. Jeperson seemed to believe that Lance had tried to pin the whole smuggling scheme on Nick. "I'll testify," he said. He felt more sadness than anything else. But Lance had made his own choices, and now he'd have to live with them. Nick wouldn't abandon him, but now Lance's life was up to Lance.

They pulled up to the house. Nick was startled to see a light on upstairs. His throat tightened with apprehension. She was supposed to be gone. Someone had delivered his keys to him today, so he'd assumed she'd moved out. She should have. After the message he'd sent, the one that had ripped him apart, she'd had two days to get away. He'd wanted her gone.

In time she'd realize that she didn't want to be anchored to someone like him—a man who had put her life in danger more than once, a man who had ended up a jailbird again, if only for two days, a man who now had a limited future, at best. He would continue to run his own small carpentry business and eke out a living here, but the city cried out for a more creative life-style than he could provide for someone like Laura.

She probably wasn't there. Maybe she'd left a light on to discourage burglars. Nick grimaced at the thought. Some protector he was, with his locks and alarm system. He'd never forget running up the stairs and finding her, her jaw already coloring where that creep had hit her, her eyes wide with terror as Robles pointed a gun at her head. When Nick remembered Robles's hand across Laura's mouth, his fingers gripping her cheek, he still shook with rage. He'd hoped the guy would make a false move so he could shoot him in good conscience, but it hadn't happened quite that way. Come to think of it, nothing had.

"Nick?"

Nick turned, startled out of his musings. They were parked at the curb and Jeperson was waiting for him to get out. "Sorry." Nick opened the car door. "I'll bet you're late for another one of Susan's excellent suppers, too." He climbed out of the car.

"She's used to it."

Nick felt a pang of envy. Jeperson had a nice family—loving wife, cute kid, another on the way. "Thanks for the lift," Nick said, leaning in and smiling at his young lawyer before he closed the door.

"Stay in touch."

"You bet. I told you, Jep, that I'm through running away from the law. Now get on home to Susan." He patted the car door and turned away. Jeperson put the car into gear.

Nick gazed at the house—his house soon. It sure looked good to him, even though he knew he still had a ton of work to do on it. He started up the walk. Someone in the neighborhood was cooking beef stew, the kind that has to simmer all day. After the food in jail, the aroma made his mouth water. He'd probably be stuck with ordering a pizza tonight, but wouldn't complain. He'd be eating it in his own house instead of a cell.

He thought of Lance, still sitting in one of those cells, and the feelings of remorse returned. They probably always would, but he'd have to fight them. Maybe imprisonment was the only thing that would change Lance's thinking. Then again, maybe even prison wouldn't do the trick.

Lance was further gone than he'd thought. Nick would keep visiting him and encourage him in any way he could. But he was through shielding his little brother. Nick had decided that he probably deserved to do some time himself for being so stupid, trying to save Lance from his own greed. Thanks to some distinguished city father, Nick had been spared that. He would have to find out who that had been and thank him.

Nick put his key into the lock. The scent of stew was close, probably right next door. Then he opened the door and the smell of savory vegetables and beef filled his nostrils. Music from an easy-listening station drifted from upstairs. His heart slammed against his chest as the realization hit him. She was still here.

Joy and hope surged through him. She was still here. He could go up those steps, take her into his arms, and... No. Laura didn't deserve a jailbird. She deserved a solid citizen, someone who had no idea how to wield a ball peen hammer as a weapon, someone safe like Jeperson. He couldn't let her make the mistake of choosing a man with a viper tattooed on his arm. Slowly he stepped inside, then closed and locked the door.

Apparently she hadn't gotten the word that he'd be coming home tonight, although Jeperson had talked with her. He might be wrong, though, because the whole business about dropping the charges had been confusing. He wasn't used to having people in high places do him favors. The opposite usually happened to him.

Every muscle, every nerve in his body strained upward, urging him to run up the stairs and hold her, kiss her.... He almost groaned aloud at the thought. Facing her, telling her she'd have to forget him, would be the hardest thing he'd ever do in his life. But he couldn't turn around and leave, either. He had nowhere to go, and besides, this was his house. If she didn't have an apartment yet, he could spend the night in Lance's room. He wondered how she'd managed to cook beef stew. He passed the kitchen. No light was on and it looked as uninhabitable as ever.

As he climbed the stairs he called her name. Didn't want to scare her. Lord knows, he'd given her enough scary experiences to last a lifetime.

"I'm here," she called back, her voice light, musical, the same voice he'd reacted to so strongly on the telephone the first time he'd heard it. He closed his eyes as longing washed over him. *I'm here.* He burned with jealousy toward the man who would finally claim her and have the luxury of hearing those two wonderful words every night when he came home. Could any man possibly appreciate that simple greeting the way he did at this moment?

He reached the top and paused. She was folding napkins and setting two places at the card table she must have found in the garage. Candles, flowers and two goblets were on the table. This was a homecoming, no doubt about it. His throat ached.

She had on a simple green dress. Her hair was loose. The bruise on her jaw was still there, but was beginning to fade. She glanced at him and smiled. "Hello, Nick." Her tone was seductive. It was a tone he remembered. She gestured toward the wineglasses. "Buy you a drink?"

He couldn't speak. How had she known such a celebration would mean so much to him, when he hadn't even known himself?

"I thought you'd like to see what your three hundred dollars bought," she said, and pirouetted so he could see the dress. "Like it?"

He nodded, still unable to speak. The dress was perfect for her, classy and sophisticated, yet sexy, too. He supposed anything she wore would seem sexy to him right now.

"Supper's almost ready." She didn't move toward him, just waited by the table, completing the picture that had him completely entranced. Behind her the lights of the city sparkled through the French doors. He hadn't realized until this moment that the setting was perfect for candlelight and wine—and a woman as beautiful as this one.

His voice came out almost as a croak. "How did you do this?" He gestured toward the table. "The whole house smells like beef stew, as if you'd been cooking it all day. But the stove doesn't work."

"There's a gizmo called a Crock-Pot."

He noticed it now on the desk. "I didn't know you could cook," he said, and realized that sounded really stupid. "I mean . . ."

"Would it make a difference if I could?" Her brown eyes flashed with amusement. "We didn't talk about that, did we? You have no idea what services I could perform around here. Maybe you shouldn't have been so quick to shovel me out the door."

"Laura, that wasn't what I was trying to do." He heard the pleading note in his voice, but desperately wanted her to understand.

"Oh?" She smoothed the pink tablecloth. She must have bought it. He didn't own any tablecloths. "Then what were you trying to do, if I may ask? I've been dying to ask, as a matter of fact. But you wouldn't let me talk to you."

She couldn't see it, yet how could she miss the contrast between them? Here he was in his disheveled, unshaven state, she in her crisp green dress and gleaming curtain of hair. "You didn't belong down there, dammit. I hated seeing you in that place, and once I knew you were out, I never wanted you back there."

Her chin lifted. "You're patronizing me again, Nick. I thought we had that settled. I'm a grown woman and I want to be treated like one."

A current of desire shot through him. He well remembered the last time she'd made such a statement to him. They'd been tucked away in a hotel room, and soon after that he'd walked into the bathroom they'd shared and . . . He shook his head. He couldn't think of that now. "I thought you'd have found an apartment by now. It would have been easier that way, for both of us."

"Just like that? You expected me to get an apartment and a job? In two days?" Her voice rose. "Who do you think I am, Superwoman?"

He gazed at her. She was magnificent. "That's who I think you are, Laura."

She tossed her head. "Well, I have the job."

"Good." He'd known she could do it.

"But the apartment's impossible."

"Oh? Are the rents too high?"

"No. It's the location."

He frowned. Okay. Practical matters. He could deal with practical matters. "Maybe I can help. Where do you want to live?"

"Right here."

It took him a second. "Laura . . ."

"With you," she finished. She placed her palms upon the table and gave him a look that reminded him with excruciating clarity of dim lights and fried chicken. "I want to marry you and live in this house," she said, her voice low and sensuous once more.

His heart thumped erratically. She was crazy. "No, you don't, Laura. You can have anybody you want. Don't settle for me. Look at me. I just got out of jail."

"Where you didn't belong. Thank goodness, Mr. Chambers agreed with me."

He was stunned. "Chambers? You don't mean . . . ?"

"P. Delwood Chambers," she said, looking smug. "He's on the museum board. I knew you'd be too proud to ask for help, but I wasn't. I went to see him last night and told him all that you did."

"Yeah." He snorted in disgust. "Kept the mask away from the authorities an extra two days."

"He understands that," she said gently. "He has a family of his own, and he knows the pressures that can make family members try to help each other, even bend the law a little."

Nick shook his head. "I still don't believe he'd intervene for me. Not P. Delwood."

"Well, he was a little tough to convince, but then Joanne agreed to come over, and—"

"Joanne? After I turned her down on the bail-bond thing?" Nick's brain was spinning.

"Joanne didn't have all the facts on you, either, Nick. But she does now, because I told her. And don't look at me like that." She folded her arms and spoke with an authority that surprised him. "It's time you gave up some of this stubborn independence and made a life for yourself."

He was taken aback. Who was she to tell him how to run his life? "But Joanne—"

"Is a fair-minded woman, when given half a chance." She studied him. "You don't look bad with a two-day-old beard, Nick."

He rubbed his chin and grinned sheepishly. "Shaving seemed beside the point."

"If you want to know, it makes you look sexy as hell."

Her eyes were like magnets in the flickering candlelight. In the face of her determination, her newfound power, he felt his resolutions slipping. "Tell me about Joanne's talk with Chambers," he said reluctantly.

"Well, she worked on him, and finally he acknowledged that he'd been a little bullheaded, and that the mask was a treasure that you'd apparently risked your life for."

"I guess you didn't mention I turned it into a missile at one point."

"No." Her eyes grew more luminous; her voice was a caress. "Although that's the moment I remember, you tossing a four-million-dollar relic around in hopes of rescuing me."

He tore his gaze away. He had to break her spell, somehow. "If I hadn't screwed up in the first place and left you alone, you wouldn't have needed rescuing. I'm glad to be out of jail, and I'm grateful for what you and Joanne did, but I really deserve to be behind bars after putting you in danger like that."

"Will you stop it?" She stormed around the table and stomped up to him. "I was afraid that was your reasoning. No, not afraid, hopeful. Because I can deal with this garbage. You were caught in an impossible situation. I encouraged you to go and talk with Lance. Stop blaming yourself! You act as if you're responsible for the whole world, and if you make one mistake, you have to pay for it forever. And another thing. Get rid of the idea that you're not good enough for me!"

"I'm not," he said, believing it even as he watched her unleash her fiery temper. She'd been sensational before; now that she had complete faith in herself she was unstoppable. Her perfume wafted tantalizingly toward him. He clenched his hands into fists to keep from touching her.

"B.S.," she said sweetly. "Now, if you really don't want me, if you think I'll be a noose around your neck, a ball and chain of a different kind than prison provides, then I'll go. I'll go right now, in a taxi, to a hotel. So answer me. Is it that you don't think you're good enough, which I won't accept as a reason, or that you're hiding behind that and really don't want me?"

He gazed into her eyes and struggled to say what should be said, to lie through his teeth and tell her he didn't want her, that she'd be an unwelcome burden, when in fact she would make his whole life worth living.

Her voice dropped to a soft murmur. "Do you swear to tell the truth, the whole truth, and nothing but the truth, so help you God?"

"Laura . . ."

"Nick, listen to me. Lots of people in your life have tried to convince you that you're worthless. You're one of the finest men I've ever known, and if I'm lucky enough to become your wife, I'll bless every day we spend together." A glint came into her eyes. "And all that aside, I crave your body like you wouldn't believe."

He felt something loosen around his heart, something that had been gripping him for a very long time. If she believed in him, maybe there was a chance he could be the man she thought he was.

"I love you, Nick Hooper," she whispered, and reached up to cradle his face in her soft hands that smelled of soap and lotion. "All I ask is that you love me back."

He groaned and gathered her close. He still couldn't quite accept that this could be happening to him, that she loved him and wanted him, but he was damn well going to try. He hoped she knew what she was doing, because once he had her in his arms, he'd never let go. "I'll love you back," he said, putting a new certainty into his words. "I'll love you back for as long as I live. I knew that the first time I kissed you." He looked into her eyes. "But until this moment I didn't have the courage to ask you to share my life. I do now. Please marry me, Laura."

She smiled a smile he would remember for the rest of his days. "Of course, I will." She molded herself against him, promising herself in a way that mere words could never do.

Gently he touched the bruise on her jaw. "But I don't know if I can ever forgive myself for putting you in danger because that damned brother of mine—"

"Hush." She rested her fingertip against his lips. "It was understandable, what you did."

He held her hand and kissed each finger before holding her hand against his cheek. "He's on his own now."

She ran her fingers lightly over his jaw. "Good." She took a deep breath. "Oh, Nick, this has been so crazy. We only met five days ago. Can you believe that?"

"No." He traced the outline of her lips and feasted on the look of love in her eyes. "But it doesn't matter.

Those five days are worth more than all the years of my life put together."

"For me, too." Tears glistened in her eyes. "What if somehow things had been different? What if we'd missed each other?"

He gazed at her, remembering the first kiss that had changed everything for both of them. Now he'd experienced the wonder of her loving, and that made his anticipation even greater. He knew how sweet her lips would taste, how delicate her skin would feel as he gently undressed her and they began their lifetime of loving.

He couldn't believe that the past five days had been an accident, that emotions so powerful had arisen from chance occurrences. "Surely you know we wouldn't have missed each other," he said, realizing it was true. He loved her with everything in him. "People as determined as we are would never have let that happen."

She smiled back. "I guess you're right." She gazed at him, her eyes darkening with passion. The pressure of her body changed subtly, becoming more fluid and welcoming against him. He felt himself responding. She ran her tongue over her top lip. "Hungry?"

Slowly, allowing this moment to impress itself forever upon his memory, he leaned forward and touched his lips to hers. "I'm starving."

HARLEQUIN Temptation

Rebels & Rogues

Quinn: He was a real-life hero to everyone except himself.

THE MIGHTY QUINN
by Candace Schuler
Temptation #397, June 1992

All men are not created equal. Some are rough around the edges. Tough-minded but tenderhearted. Incredibly sexy. The tempting fulfillment of every woman's fantasy.

When it's time to fight for what they believe in, to win that special woman, our Rebels and Rogues are heroes at heart. Twelve Rebels and Rogues, one each month in 1992, only from Harlequin Temptation!

Harlequin®

JANELLE TAYLOR

Valley of Fire

HARLEQUIN IS PROUD TO PRESENT *VALLEY OF FIRE* BY JANELLE TAYLOR—AUTHOR OF TWENTY-TWO BOOKS, INCLUDING SIX *NEW YORK TIMES* BESTSELLERS

VALLEY OF FIRE—the warm and passionate story of Kathy Alexander, a famous romance author, and Steven Winngate, entrepreneur and owner of the magazine that intended to expose the real Kathy ''Brandy'' Alexander to her fans.

Don't miss VALLEY OF FIRE, available in May.

OVER THE YEARS, TELEVISION HAS BROUGHT
THE LIVES AND LOVES OF MANY CHARACTERS INTO
YOUR HOMES. NOW HARLEQUIN INTRODUCES YOU
TO THE TOWN AND PEOPLE OF

One small town—twelve terrific love stories.

GREAT READING...GREAT SAVINGS...AND A FABULOUS
FREE GIFT!

Each book set in Tyler is a self-contained love story; together, the
twelve novels stitch the fabric of the community.

By collecting proofs-of-purchase found in each Tyler book, you can
receive a fabulous gift, ABSOLUTELY FREE! And use our special
Tyler coupons to save on your next TYLER book purchase.

Join us for the fourth TYLER book,
MONKEY WRENCH by Nancy Martin.

*Can elderly Rose Atkins successfully bring a new love into
granddaughter Susannah's life?*

FREE GIFT OFFER

To receive your free gift, send us the specified number of proofs-of-purchase from any specially marked Free Gift Offer Harlequin or Silhouette book with the Free Gift Certificate properly completed, plus a check or money order (do not send cash) to cover postage and handling payable to Harlequin/Silhouette Free Gift Promotion Offer. We will send you the specified gift.

FREE GIFT CERTIFICATE

ITEM	A. GOLD TONE EARRINGS	B. GOLD TONE BRACELET	C. GOLD TONE NECKLACE
# of proofs-of-purchase required	3	6	9
Postage and Handling	$2.25	$2.75	$3.25
Check one	☐	☐	☐

Name: _____

Address: _____

City: _____ Province: _____ Postal Code: _____

Mail this certificate, specified number of proofs-of-purchase and a check or money order for postage and handling to: HARLEQUIN/SILHOUETTE FREE GIFT OFFER 1992, P.O. Box 622, Fort Erie, Ontario L2A 5X3. Requests must be received by July 31, 1992.

PLUS—Every time you submit a completed certificate with the correct number of proofs-of-purchase, you are automatically entered in our MILLION DOLLAR SWEEPSTAKES! No purchase or obligation necessary to enter. See below for alternate means of entry and how to obtain complete sweepstakes rules.

MILLION DOLLAR SWEEPSTAKES
NO PURCHASE OR OBLIGATION NECESSARY TO ENTER

To enter, hand-print (mechanical reproductions are not acceptable) your name and address on a 3″×5″ card and mail to Million Dollar Sweepstakes 6097, c/o either P.O. Box 9056, Buffalo, NY 14269-9056 or P.O. Box 621, Fort Erie, Ontario L2A 5X3. Limit: one entry per envelope. Entries must be sent via 1st-class mail. For eligibility, entries must be received no later than March 31, 1994. No liability is assumed for printing errors, lost, late or misdirected entries.

Sweepstakes is open to persons 18 years of age or older. All applicable laws and regulations apply. Sweepstakes offer void wherever prohibited by law. Prizewinners will be determined no later than May 1994. Chances of winning are determined by the number of entries distributed and received. For a copy of the Official Rules governing this sweepstakes offer, send a self-addressed, stamped envelope (WA residents need not affix return postage) to: Million Dollar Sweepstakes Rules, P.O. Box 4733, Blair, NE 68009.

HT2C

ONE PROOF-OF-PURCHASE
To collect your fabulous FREE GIFT you must include the necessary FREE GIFT proofs-of-purchase with a properly completed offer certificate.

(See inside back cover for offer details)